BL 4.8
8520

FELICIA
the Critic

by Ellen Conford

Little, Brown and Company
Boston · Toronto · London

The characters and events in this book are fictitious. Any similarity to real persons, living
or dead, is coincidental and not intended by the author.

Library of Congress Cataloging-in-Publication Data

Conford, Ellen.
    Felicia the critic.
    SUMMARY: Felicia's constant criticising gets her
into trouble even though she tries to be constructive.
ISBN 0-316-15295-1 (hc)
ISBN 0-316-15358-3 (pb)
    I. Stewart, Arvis L., illus. (hc)   II. Title.
PZ7.C7593Fe   [Fic]   73-7831

                 10 9 8 7 6 5 4 3 2 1

MV-NY

Published simultaneously in Canada
by Little, Brown & Company (Canada) Limited

Printed in the United States of America

To Susan Pfeffer
and to David and Michael

FELICIA
the Critic

1

". . . and the current temperature is forty-nine W G V M degrees."

Felicia looked at the thermometer outside the kitchen window and shook her head.

"The current temperature is fifty-one K E R S H-E N B A U M degrees," she informed the radio announcer, who was now doing a commercial for Al's Auto Agency.

"Do we *have* to go through this *every morning?*" moaned her sister Marilyn.

"Have to go through what every morning?" asked Felicia, sprinkling sugar over her cold cereal.

"Felicia!" Her mother grabbed her hand as she dipped into the sugar bowl for the fourth time. "Three spoonfuls is enough!"

"*I'm* not on a diet," Felicia said, watching Marilyn shell a hard-boiled egg. "Have to go through what every morning?" she repeated.

"Marilyn," their father began, "you're not eating

3

enough to keep an ant alive. You will perish of malnutrition in a house with a fifteen-cubic-foot refrigerator. How long are you going to stay on this idiotic diet?"

"Every morning," Marilyn said to Felicia, "you listen to the weather forecast and say it's wrong."

"But it always is," Felicia insisted.

"Does it seem as if Marilyn's ignoring me?" Mr. Kershenbaum asked Mrs. Kershenbaum.

"It does seem that way, yes," she replied.

"Did it ever occur to you," Marilyn demanded, "that *you* might be wrong?"

"No," said Felicia.

Marilyn drummed her fingers on the table. Felicia knew that meant that Marilyn was getting very angry, but she couldn't understand what she was angry about.

"Look," Marilyn began, trying to sound very patient, but not sounding patient at all, "if it *annoys* you so much that they always have the temperature wrong, *why* do you always *listen?*"

"Because I like to know what the weather's going to be," explained Felicia. Why else would you listen to the weather forecast, she wondered. Sometimes Marilyn couldn't seem to understand the simplest things.

"But if you — "

"Marilyn! Enough, please," their mother interrupted, holding up her hand. "It's much too early for this."

"Are you going to eat anything besides that hard-boiled egg?" Mr. Kershenbaum asked.

"May I have a cup of black coffee?" Marilyn asked.

"No, you may not!" her mother retorted.

"Then I'm not eating anything besides the egg," Marilyn told her father.

"Did you know that black coffee will rot your liver faster than liquor?" Felicia informed them.

"Felicia, please!" said her mother, putting down her coffee cup.

"Actually," said Felicia, hoping she hadn't really scared her mother, "I don't even remember where I read that. I just didn't want Marilyn to feel bad because she couldn't have coffee. Maybe I just now made it up."

"I can't stand it!" Marilyn cried, pushing her chair back from the table.

She means she can't stand me, Felicia thought. No matter what Felicia said or did these days, Marilyn couldn't seem to stand her. The thing is, her mother had said, Marilyn is thirteen, and very sensitive. As if that explained anything! Why did being sensitive give you the right to be nasty to other people? Who might, Felicia thought resentfully, be sensitive too.

"You know," Felicia began helpfully, eyeing Marilyn's bright red sweater and white slacks, and thinking of how concerned her sister was about her looks these days, "they say that dark colors make you seem thinner."

"Ohhh!" sputtered Marilyn and stalked out of the kitchen without another word.

"Felicia," her mother sighed.

"What?" asked Felicia, completely bewildered. She had made a simple suggestion about how her sister could look thinner — and wasn't that what Marilyn wanted, or why else would she be on a diet? — and Marilyn was mad at her again.

"Forget it," her father said hopelessly.

"Can I wear my reindeer sweater?" Felicia asked, jumping up from the table.

"Oh, I think it's a little chilly for just your sweater," her mother objected.

"Oh, no it's not, please, it's fifty-one degrees," Felicia pleaded. Her aunt had knitted her a beautiful blue-and-white sweater, and she had been waiting for over a month for the weather to be just right — not too warm and not too cold. "I'll be too hot in my winter coat. *Please!*"

"All right, all right," her mother gave in.

Felicia ran upstairs and flung open the door of her closet. The sweater was still in its box, carefully nestled in white tissue paper. Felicia lovingly stroked the fuzzy wool, and unfolded it so she could hold it up in front of the mirror. She slipped it on over her head, and smoothed it down in front.

Beautiful!

She stepped back to look at herself. She turned around as gracefully as she could, in front of the mirror. She couldn't see the back of herself as she turned, but it was what people always did when they admired clothes that they were trying on.

She ran downstairs and grabbed her books and her lunch.

"I'm going!" she yelled to her parents.

"Wait, let's see how you look in the sweater!" her mother called.

"Isn't it beautiful?" Felicia beamed as her parents came to the door to see her off.

She turned around again so they could admire both sides of her.

"It really is," her mother agreed.

" 'Bye," she said, hugging her mother.

"Have a good day," her father said.

Felicia was sure it would be a good day. She was wearing her sweater at last, and Cheryl was going to meet her at the corner, so she was sure she would have someone to walk to school with. Sometimes

Cheryl's father drove her to school, like when she had to bring her bass viol in for orchestra, and then Felicia often ended up walking alone.

Sometimes girls she knew would say, "Hi, Felicia," and that meant she could walk with them, but some days nobody said, "Hi, Felicia," and she had to walk by herself.

It wasn't that she didn't like to walk by herself. Lots of times, after school or during vacations, she went on walks alone, exploring blocks beyond her own, hoping that she would have some sort of adventure, or maybe even discover a completely uncharted, brand-new block that no one had ever seen before. (She hadn't discovered one as yet, and she didn't really think it was very likely that she would, but you never know.)

But somehow, walking to school alone was different from taking a walk.

Cheryl was not at the corner when Felicia got there. Felicia felt her stomach skitter with disappointment. Maybe Mr. Sweet had driven her to school after all. Or maybe Cheryl was sick, and not even coming to school today.

Felicia suddenly felt a little chilly under her sweater, and she shivered. Maybe she'd been wrong; maybe it wasn't a beautiful sweater day at all.

Then she saw Cheryl trotting up Decatur Street toward the corner. Felicia felt such a wave of relief wash over her that she wanted to grab Cheryl and hug her.

But instead she said, "You're late."

"Well, I couldn't help it," Cheryl panted, sounding a little annoyed. "I woke up late and my mother made me practice a whole half-hour anyway."

They started up Perry Street, walking slowly so Cheryl could catch her breath.

"If you got an alarm clock," Felicia suggested, "you could wake up on time."

"I have an alarm clock," Cheryl said. "I forgot to set it."

"Maybe if you put a little sign next to it, like, 'REMEMBER TO SET ME' or something — "

"For heaven's sake, Felicia," Cheryl broke in, "this is the first time in a whole year I overslept." She still sounded annoyed. She must be mad at her mother for making her practice even though she was late, Felicia thought. That *is* pretty unreasonable.

But that was the way Mrs. Sweet was. Not unreasonable — in fact, Mrs. Sweet thought herself *very* reasonable. She talked in a cool, reasonable tone of voice, and everything she said was reasonable. But she made Cheryl *do* a lot of things, and Cheryl wasn't sure she wanted to do all of them.

Like taking ballet lessons and going to the French class at the Saturday morning Cultural Arts Community Workshop, and taking ice-skating lessons and having to practice the bass viol.

Although the bass really was a victory for Cheryl. Mrs. Sweet had wanted her to learn viola or violin in school, but once Cheryl saw the bass viol and heard the sounds it made, she was determined not to be talked out of it. And she had won. But since she had to practice a half hour every day, Felicia wasn't sure if she had really won anything.

They walked the rest of the way to school without saying very much, but that was all right. Felicia loved to talk, but sometimes Cheryl didn't. And it didn't matter, because they were friends. They could walk together without saying one word, and that was okay with Felicia.

The crossing guard stopped them just as they stepped off the curb to cross the street.

"Hold it there!" he ordered.

Felicia and Cheryl stepped back onto the sidewalk.

"Look at that," grumbled Felicia. "He's letting all those cars go by, and then he's going to let the other cars make their turns, and there are only two of us standing here, and we were practically halfway across the street anyway."

"It doesn't seem fair," Cheryl agreed.

"It's not just that it's not fair," Felicia complained,

"but it's not *efficient*, either." "Efficient" had become one of Felicia's favorite words, ever since her father had pointed out to her that there were more *efficient* ways of getting her room cleaned up than by throwing everything into the bottom of her closet and then hoping that her mother wouldn't tell her she had to clean out the closet.

"The efficient way would be to let us cross because there are only two of us, and then let those three cars turn, and then the traffic going straight wouldn't have to stop at all after that. Because," Felicia glanced nervously around, "I think we're the last ones here."

The policeman stopped the traffic again, and waved the two girls across the street.

"You see," Felicia said, hurrying into the school yard, "he just had to stop another whole line of cars to let us cross. Not efficient."

"Hurry up," urged Cheryl, sounding annoyed again. "We're going to be late."

At lunchtime, Felicia and Cheryl sat at a table with Phyllis Brody, Lorraine Kalman and Fern Krinsky.

"Look at that Wendy Frank," Phyllis whispered. "Talking about her club. That's all she ever does. What's so great about her old club anyway?"

"What's so great about *any* club?" Felicia asked.

Phyllis looked at her disdainfully.

"Well, what do they do?" Felicia wanted to know. "What's the club for?"

"For?" echoed Fern. "What does it have to be for? It's a *club*."

"Well, shouldn't it be *for* something?" Felicia persisted. "You know, like stamp collectors, or ecology, or to feed starving children?"

"It's just a club, Felicia," Lorraine said, in the same patient-but-not-really-patient tone of voice Marilyn often used with her.

"I think a club should be to *do* something," Felicia went on doggedly. "Or else it's not a club, it's just a *group*."

Phyllis and Lorraine exchanged looks.

"*Anyway*," Phyllis continued, glaring at Felicia, "the way she's always whispering to people makes me sick."

"Maybe it wouldn't make you sick if she whispered to you sometimes," Felicia suggested, tearing open her bag of corn chips.

Phyllis scowled at her. "Eat your corn chips, Felicia," she said coldly.

But Phyllis's anger made Felicia's stomach jump. She pushed the cellophane bag to the center of the table. "Anybody want some?" she muttered, without looking up at the girls.

Nobody answered her, but Phyllis and Lorraine and Fern helped themselves to generous handfuls of the corn chips.

"Felicia, want to trade?" Cheryl asked. "I have bologna."

"Thanks," Felicia said gratefully. Cheryl always sensed the right thing to say.

"Here." Felicia handed Cheryl half of her sandwich.

Cheryl grinned. "But you have bologna too."

"But yours is on rye bread, and mine is on whole wheat," Felicia explained.

That wasn't really the reason. Felicia liked whole wheat bread almost as much as rye. She just wanted to trade with Cheryl today.

It made her feel better.

2

"Where's Mom?" Felicia asked, dropping her school books on the kitchen table.

"Shopping," said Marilyn, not even looking up from her fingernails, which she was gloomily painting "Concord Grape."

Felicia opened the refrigerator door and peered inside.

"A good thing she is," commented Felicia, rummaging around through the shelves. "There isn't a thing in here to eat."

She took two slices of American cheese and a square of semisweet baking chocolate and put them on the table, along with a jar of peanut butter from the cabinet, and a spoon.

"You're going to get pimples if you keep on eating like that," Marilyn predicted.

Felicia took a spoonful of peanut butter and licked at it.

"Yecch," grimaced Marilyn. "How can you? Just watching you eat that makes me ill."

"Don't watch me, then," said Felicia reasonably.

"What do you think of this color?" Marilyn asked, holding up her hand so Felicia could see her nails.

The question was so unexpected that Felicia was startled. Marilyn never asked her opinion about anything, and half the time when Felicia said something to her sister, the reply was, "Who asked you?"

Felicia carefully peeled the plastic wrap off her cheese. Did Marilyn want to know the truth, or was she going to be sensitive and hurt if Felicia said she didn't like the color? Felicia sat, nibbling her cheese, hoping Marilyn would forget she'd asked.

"What do you think of this color?" Marilyn repeated irritably. "Aren't you listening?"

"I'm listening," Felicia said calmly.

"*Well?*"

"I think," Felicia said reluctantly, "that it looks like dried blood."

"Ohh!" Marilyn hissed. "You — "

Felicia jerked away from her sister, who looked as if she were about to lunge at her, and her arm hit the peanut butter jar, knocking it off the table to the floor, where it made a splattering smash.

"Ohh," groaned Felicia, looking at the mess of

broken glass and peanut butter scattered over the kitchen.

"You'd better clean that up before Mother gets home," Marilyn warned. Felicia thought her sister looked almost glad about the mess on the floor.

Felicia went to the broom closet to get the broom and dustpan. The narrow closet was a jumble of cleaning equipment, all looking as if it would tumble out at you if you tried to remove anything. Felicia tugged at the broom, catching a sponge mop as it fell out at her and shoving it back in the closet. The dustpan was on the floor, with a pail of rags and a can of floor wax on top of it. Assorted spray cans, jars and containers surrounded it on all sides. Carefully Felicia maneuvered things around till she could get the dustpan out.

"Whew," she breathed, forcing the closet door shut and leaning against it, "I'm tired before I've even started. What an inefficient closet."

She started to sweep up the shattered glass, but it was all mixed in with the peanut butter and Felicia realized she was smearing the stuff all over the floor.

"Oh!" she wailed. "Look at this!"

Marilyn looked disinterestedly. "You're making a bigger mess than before," she remarked.

The front door opened. "It's me," their mother called.

"Don't come in here with bare feet!" yelled Felicia.

"I don't usually go shopping in my bare — what happened here?" Mrs. Kershenbaum asked, standing in the kitchen doorway with two bags of groceries in her arms.

"It was an accident," Felicia said. "And I'm not doing too well getting it cleaned up."

"I can see that. Marilyn, take these bags, please, and be careful not to slip. I have three more out in the car you can help me with."

Marilyn sighed deeply and pulled herself up from her chair with a great effort. She took the bags from her mother and put them on the kitchen table.

"Wait, Felicia, I'll help you with that," her mother said. "I think you're just making it worse. Marilyn what *is* that on your fingernails?"

"Concord Grape," Marilyn said.

"Remove it, please," her mother said. "You look like a vampire."

"*Mother*," Marilyn began, in her most exasperated voice.

"I thought it looked like dried blood," Felicia said.

"Maybe that's why I thought of a vampire," her mother mused.

"*Mother*," Marilyn repeated.

"Oh, forget it, Marilyn," her mother said. "Leave

it on, leave it on. If you want to look like a vampire, that's your business. Just help me get those groceries in, please."

Grumbling, Marilyn followed her out to the car. They came back in and plopped the bags down on the table.

"We'd better get this cleaned up first," said Mrs. Kershenbaum, taking off her coat, "or we'll kill ourselves."

She opened the broom closet door, and the mop fell out at her. She shoved it back in and pulled out a bag of sponges.

"Look, do it this way," she said, showing Felicia how to push the glass into one heap with the sponge and then wipe it all into the dustpan. "See, with the sponge you won't cut yourself and then when the glass is all cleaned up you can take care of the peanut butter."

"There," she said when Felicia was finished, "now we can walk in here without risk to life and limb. Where did Marilyn go? I wanted her to help me put the groceries away."

"Don't call her," Felicia said quickly. "I'll help you." She wanted an excuse to be alone with her mother. The way Phyllis, Lorraine and Fern had talked to her at lunch had bothered Felicia all day.

Even walking home with Cheryl hadn't made her forget the way she felt when Phyllis said, "Eat your corn chips, Felicia," in that cold, disdainful voice. Maybe her mother could explain why the girls had acted that way.

"So," Mrs. Kershenbaum said briskly when Felicia finished telling her the conversation as exactly as she could remember, "you got the feeling they were mad at you."

"It was no feeling," Felicia said positively. "They were mad at me, all right. But I don't know why."

Her mother looked at her for a long time. "Are you sure," she said finally, "you don't know why? You haven't even got an idea?"

"Well," Felicia hesitated, "I told the truth. Maybe they didn't like that."

"Felicia," her mother said gently, "there's a difference between truth and opinion. The truth is facts. Opinion is what you think. You told them what you thought."

"And they didn't like that. Shouldn't I say what I think?"

Her mother frowned. "Look, if you have a great idea for something and someone comes along and says, 'Boy, what a dumb idea, this is wrong and this is wrong,' wouldn't you feel bad?"

"I guess so," Felicia said uncertainly.

"Well, you see, you tend to be a little — critical. People don't like it when you tell them all their bad points, or all the things that are wrong with their ideas."

"It's bad to be critical?" asked Felicia, puzzled.

"Not that it's bad," her mother said. "But don't expect people to like it when you tell them what they're doing wrong, or why their plans won't work. Actually, there are people who make a career out of being critical."

"There are?"

"Sure. Critics."

"What do they do?" Felicia asked curiously.

"They read books and see plays and movies and concerts and television shows, and then they write their opinions about them. They explain what they thought was wrong and what they thought was right."

Felicia thought about this for a minute. Her mother said she tended to be critical, and there were actually people who got paid for being critical! Maybe . . .

"Maybe *I'll* be a critic some day," Felicia said thoughtfully.

"I wouldn't be surprised," her mother grinned. "But, in the meanwhile, you might try constructive criticism."

"Constructive criticism?"

"Instead of saying, 'This is lousy, this is lousy and this is lousy,' you point out how it could be better. See, constructive criticism is helpful. If you just tear something apart, you're being destructive. But if you show how it could be made better or done better, you're being constructive. And that's a very valuable talent to have, to be able to be a constructive critic."

A constructive critic! thought Felicia. That's what she was going to be from now on. Her parents always said that a child should develop his talents. A gift shouldn't be neglected, they said. It should be nourished, and practiced, till you got better and better at it.

Well, Felicia decided, criticalness is my talent, and I ought to develop it. There is no point, her mother always advised Marilyn, in trying to be something you're not. Just be the best you can at what you are.

That's what I'll do, Felicia resolved. I'll be the best critic I can. Constructive critic, she reminded herself.

"Do you mind," Felicia asked her mother, "if I make some constructive criticisms about the broom closet?"

"What?" asked her mother, perplexed.

"Well, I just decided I'm going to be a constructive critic and I think there might be some ways to make the broom closet more — efficient."

"Be my guest," her mother smiled. "Any constructive criticism about *that* disaster area will be appreciated."

Felicia ran to get a magazine she had seen a couple of days ago. There was a picture in it of a "cleaning closet" that she remembered. Now if she could make her mother's broom closet look like that . . .

She found the picture she wanted and studied it for a while.

Then she took a pencil and paper, and biting her lip in concentration, began to scribble down her ideas.

"Now," she announced to her mother a while later, "I have here some suggestions about the broom closet. Some constructive criticism."

"Not right now, dear," Mrs. Kershenbaum said absently, running her finger down the cookbook index.

"Then can I do what I wrote on the list myself?"

"Yes, go ahead," her mother nodded.

"I need some nails and a hammer."

"In the basement."

Felicia got hammer and nails and took everything out of the broom closet.

"Look at this," her mother said angrily. "Just look at this! A four-pound roast, and a pound of it must be fat. They had it wrapped so you could only see the top and all the fat is on the bottom."

She put the meat in a big bowl and poured wine and oil all over it.

"Why don't you take it back?" Felicia said, standing in the broom closet and making little marks on the walls with a pencil.

"Oh, it's too much trouble," her mother grumbled. "Anyway, I want it for tomorrow, and it has to be marinated overnight."

Felicia started hammering.

"What are you doing?" her mother asked.

"Putting nails in to hang things up," Felicia replied.

"Oh. Well, be careful," she said dubiously.

"What is that UNGODLY NOISE?" Marilyn yelled from the stairs.

"Felicia is fixing up the broom closet," her mother yelled back over the noise of the pounding hammer.

"She'll probably break it," Marilyn said sourly, standing at the kitchen door to watch her sister.

"You can't break a broom closet," Felicia muttered, concentrating on her project.

"*You* could," retorted Marilyn. "Which one do you like best?" she asked her mother, holding up one hand with four fingernails painted different colors.

"That one," said her mother, pointing to the one pale fingernail on Marilyn's hand.

"I didn't put any polish on that one!" Marilyn

wailed.

"Yes. I like that," her mother said firmly.

Felicia worked for almost an hour. When she was finished she stood back to survey the job. It's good, Felicia thought warmly. It's really good! It's neat, and organized and — *efficient*. She closed the door of the closet.

"I'm done," she announced. "Everybody come look."

Her father had come home while she was working and came into the kitchen now to see what she'd been doing.

"I'm here," her mother said, turning away from the stove to look.

"You too, Marilyn!" Felicia yelled.

"I do not have a consuming interest in broom closets!" Marilyn yelled back. "Hold the unveiling without me."

"Come on, Marilyn," Felicia insisted. "You were the one who said I'd break the closet."

"Oh, for heaven's sake," Marilyn complained, but she came, finally, into the kitchen too.

"Ready?" Felicia asked. "Da dum!" She flung open the door of the broom closet.

"It's gorgeous!" her mother gasped. "Felicia, it's wonderful."

24

"This is not our broom closet," declared Mr. Kershenbaum. "This is definitely not the broom closet I know and hate."

Felicia had put nails in the walls to hang up all the mops and brooms that had hooks on their handles. The ones that didn't have hooks hung with their handles downward on the wall, with two nails forming a sort of holder for them. The dustpan was also hung on a nail, and the pail, empty now, was hung by its wire carrying handle. The cleaning supplies, bottles, cans, were neatly arranged on the floor of the closet and the sponges were evenly stacked on the one small shelf at the top. Felicia had folded all the rags and put them on the shelf next to the sponges.

"I can't get over it," her mother marveled. "I've been meaning to do something about that closet for years . . ."

Felicia beamed with pride.

"Would you say that was constructive?" she asked her mother.

"Extremely."

This is a good start, Felicia thought happily. I'm going to make a fine critic.

After dinner, still glowing with the success of her broom closet project, Felicia went upstairs to her room and took out an old notebook. She tore all the used pages out of it and wrote on the first clean page: *Criticism Notebook.* She turned the page and wrote at the top of the next page: *Constructive Criticisms.*

Then she sat with her chin in her hand, nibbling on the end of her pen, thinking. She thought for quite a while, frowning with concentration, unaware of anything but the problem she was working on.

Finally, with a satisfied sigh, she bent over her notebook and began to write.

3

It was raining the next morning when Felicia came down to breakfast. The radio announcer was saying, ". . . and outside our W G V M studio the weather is: Wet."

"Care to argue with that, Felicia?" Marilyn asked, sounding almost as if she wanted a fight.

"I haven't said anything!" Felicia cried indignantly.

"Marilyn," her mother warned, "don't start. Just don't start."

Felicia shook the cereal box. Six Rice Krispies dribbled into her bowl.

"Oh, well," she said cheerfully, going to the refrigerator, "I'd rather have a salami sandwich, anyway."

"Don't anybody say a word," Mr. Kershenbaum ordered, staring hard at Marilyn.

Marilyn popped the last of her hard-boiled egg into her mouth.

"I'm not saying a thing," she said, after a few swallows, "but I don't have to sit here and watch it."

She got up and left the kitchen. Her mother sighed.

"Would you like me to drive you today?" her father asked as Felicia sliced salami and spread mustard on her sandwich.

"No, I think I'll walk."

"But Felicia, it's pouring," her mother objected.

Felicia glanced out the window. "It's not really pouring," she said. "It's more like steady drizzling."

"The weather report said it was going to be raining all morning."

"Well, you know how unreliable they are," Felicia said, biting into her sandwich. "I guess I can't have any Coke with this, right?"

"Don't talk with your mouth full. And no, you can't. Take some milk."

"I'm not thirsty," Felicia said.

"Maybe Marilyn wants a ride," her father said half-heartedly.

Felicia finished her sandwich and went to get her things together for school. On her desk were two pieces of paper, which Felicia placed carefully inside the front cover of her spelling book. She stuck her books inside a plastic zipper envelope that her father had gotten for her from his office, making sure the spelling book was on top, where she could easily reach it when she needed her papers.

She ran downstairs and got her slicker and rain hat

from the front closet. The slicker was bright red and the hat was white with a shiny plastic finish and red polka dots. Felicia didn't much like the slicker, even though it was what a lot of the kids wore, because it made her hot and sticky after a while, but she loved the hat, which had a floppy brim and tied under her chin. Felicia thought she looked very nice in the hat, but that wasn't the reason she was so eager to walk to school in the rain today.

She went into the kitchen to get her lunch.

"What did you make me?" she asked her mother, taking the brown paper bag from the refrigerator.

"A salami sandwich," her mother said.

"But I had that for breakfast!" Felicia exclaimed.

"Believe me, dear," her mother said, "if I had had the slightest notion that you were going to — "

"Oh, don't worry," Felicia brightened. "It really doesn't matter. I love salami." Wasn't it silly to get upset over unimportant things, when this morning was the start of Felicia's career as a constructive critic!

" 'Bye," she said, kissing her mother on the cheek.

" 'Bye, honey."

Felicia picked up her plastic envelope and opened the front door.

"Boots!" her mother yelled from the kitchen. "Felicia!"

"Rats!" Felicia sighed and hauled her boots out of

the front closet. They were duck boots and they weren't colorful or anything, like Phyllis's red ones, and Felicia thought they made her look dopey.

"Better luck next time," Marilyn said airily, squeezing past Felicia and out the front door.

"Are you wearing your boots?" her mother called.

"I'm wearing my stupid boots!" Felicia yelled back. "Good-bye!"

"Good-bye," Felicia muttered, and closed the front door behind her.

Her father was warming up the car in the driveway as Felicia started down the walk.

"Are you sure?" he asked her, rolling down the car window.

"Positive!" Felicia called back, waving her lunch at him. She was cheerful now, forgetting almost instantly about having to wear boots, and concentrating on the important business ahead of her.

At the corner of Decatur Street a figure in a white trench coat and white rain hat was huddled under an umbrella.

"Cheryl!" Felicia shouted happily. She'd never expected Cheryl's mother to let her walk to school in the drizzle, and Felicia clumped toward her as fast as her boots would allow.

She ducked under Cheryl's umbrella.

"My father's car wouldn't start," Cheryl explained

as they started up Perry Street. "My mother wanted to call a taxi but I wouldn't let her."

"Gee, that's great!" Felicia exclaimed. Having Cheryl along to watch her in her first public role as a constructive critic was like a wonderful, unexpected bonus.

"I don't think it's so great," Cheryl said. "I don't like to walk in the rain. But I certainly wasn't going to come to school in a *taxi*."

"Listen, Cheryl," Felicia began eagerly, "I want to tell you something. When we get to — "

The honking of a horn interrupted her.

"Want a ride? Come on!" Phyllis had her head stuck out the car window. Lorraine was sitting next to her in the back seat and Mrs. Brody was driving.

"Yes!" Cheryl yelled, struggling to close her umbrella. "Come on, Felicia."

Felicia hung back, a wave of disappointment washing over her.

She held Cheryl's arm. "No, listen, Cheryl, let's walk. I have to — "

"Don't be stupid!" Cheryl snapped. "Why should we walk in the rain if we can get a ride?"

"It's not a rain," Felicia said desperately, "it's more like a steady drizzle — "

"Felicia, I'm getting soaked in this steady drizzle! Now, come on!"

"But Cheryl, I wanted to tell you — I have to — "

"Are you coming or aren't you?" Phyllis yelled impatiently.

"We're coming!" Cheryl called.

Felicia sighed. "All right," she agreed reluctantly. "But I'm going to get out a block before school." Cheryl didn't even hear her.

They got into the car, Felicia in the front seat next to Phyllis's mother and Cheryl in the back.

"Thanks," Cheryl said gratefully. "You're a lifesaver."

"That's a beautiful raincoat, Cheryl," Lorraine said. "Is it new?"

"Yes, my mother got it for me just last week. She said the plastic slicker was too hot and made me sweat too much."

Felicia noticed Mrs. Brody's nose twitching as if she smelled something vaguely unpleasant.

"Would you let me off here, please?" Felicia said softly as they reached the corner of Perry and Halsey.

"But Felicia, we're still a block from school," said Mrs. Brody, puzzled.

"Well, it's just sort of drizzling, and I really want to walk the rest of the way." She was disappointed about Cheryl and her slicker was beginning to feel stickily uncomfortable.

All the excitement seemed to have gone out of her,

leaving her feeling like a deflated balloon. Lorraine and Phyllis were admiring Cheryl's new outfit, and Cheryl, who usually let her mother do all the thinking about clothes, wasn't even trying to get Felicia to join the conversation.

"Please," she said, putting her hand on the door handle.

"All right," Mrs. Brody said doubtfully. "If you're sure — "

"Thank you very much for the ride," said Felicia, climbing out of the car.

She trudged up the street toward school as Mrs. Brody drove on. Traffic was heavy now, with a line of cars and school buses inching up the street. On rainy days it was always like this, and very soon Felicia passed Mrs. Brody's car, stuck in traffic and not moving.

Felicia felt inside her plastic envelope for her spelling book and her fingers groped inside the covers to feel the two pieces of paper she'd put in there. Reassuringly she kept her fingers on the papers as she approached the school crossing.

Felicia waited with a cluster of others for the crossing guard to wave her on. Finally he held up his hand to stop the flow of traffic and signaled to the walkers.

They scurried across the street, heads bent against the rain, the little ones with book bags and lunch boxes clunking against their knees as they trotted.

Felicia stopped in the middle of the street next to the crossing guard and drew out her papers from the spelling book.

"Move along," he said. "Let's go."

"I'd like to talk to you," Felicia began politely.

"Now? What is it?"

"I have some suggestions here — "

"Suggestions!" he roared. "Are you kidding?"

"No," Felicia said, feeling a little hurt. "Of course not. Now, I have a diagram — " Horns began honking as Felicia handed a piece of paper to the crossing guard. "You see, here is the school, and here is the — "

"Get moving!" the guard shouted. "You're holding up traffic!"

Felicia, trying to keep calm, plunged ahead with what she had to say. "Well, if you'd just look at this list of suggestions, and this diagram, you'll — "

"Will you MOVE!" he howled.

Now there were cars stretching in huge lines on all three sides of the intersection, and Felicia thought that every one of them must be honking its horn. The noise was nearly deafening, so Felicia practically had to scream to be heard.

"Would you at least take these and look at them?"

Felicia shouted desperately, thrusting her papers into the policeman's hand.

He glanced at the list of suggestions. Felicia had spent almost all last evening neatly writing them out on her memo pad, which had "From the Desk of Felicia Kershenbaum" printed on the top.

He stuffed the list and the diagram into his raincoat pocket.

"Anything!" he shouted over the noise of the cars and the yelling of the children at the corner, who were waiting to get across the street. "Anything, if you'll just get away from me!"

"Thank you," Felicia said meekly, not even sure he could hear her. School bus drivers were leaning out of their windows shouting at the policeman. The horns were now a steady blare, as if everybody had decided to lean on his horn permanently, without ever letting up. The rain had begun to come down hard, so that even Felicia had to admit it was not drizzle any more, but full-fledged rain.

The crowd of children on the corner started to cross the street without waiting for the guard to direct them. At the same time, one of the school buses began to turn into the driveway of the school yard, even though the traffic guard had not signaled for it to go ahead, and another school bus, coming out of the driveway, came to a screeching halt just in time to keep from hitting the bus full of children.

Felicia thought that this would be a good time to get across the street. It was going to take the crossing guard a long time to get that snarl of cars, buses and children untangled. Felicia hoped he would read her suggestions and study her diagram. He really needed them, she thought ruefully, for he certainly was not a very efficient traffic manager.

Felicia was in art class later that morning, trying to draw how she felt.

Ms. De Mara, their art teacher, had put on a record and told them to draw what the music made them feel. Felicia liked Ms. De Mara, but she wished that every once in a while Ms. De Mara would put a bowl of fruit on her desk and say, "Draw this." Felicia could sketch pretty well if someone told her what to sketch, but thinking up something to draw was sometimes very difficult.

But Ms. De Mara had her own ideas about teaching art, and they were often quite different from the ideas of the other teachers Felicia had had.

So Felicia sat, with pastels and charcoal on her desk, and listened to the music. It was slow, and sort of sad, and it didn't actually make her feel *anything*. She drew one wavy line on her paper with a blue pastel, and then drew another wavy line underneath it. She let her arm sort of sway with the rhythm of the music as she drew the lines, but that was really about all the feeling she could work up for Ms. De Mara's assignment.

"That's very good," said Ms. De Mara, looking over Felicia's shoulder. "A good start. You really seem to have the flow of the music there."

"Thank you," Felicia murmured, worried that Ms. De Mara thought it was a good start. Felicia had thought she was finished. Was she supposed to do more?

"Just keep at it, class," the teacher said. "I'll be right back."

As soon as Ms. De Mara was out of the room, Felicia felt a sharp jab between her shoulder blades. She turned around to Phyllis, who sat behind her.

"What were you doing out there this morning?" Phyllis asked.

Felicia looked at her blankly.

"This morning," repeated Phyllis impatiently. "With that traffic cop."

"Oh," Felicia said. "Oh, yeah. Just — talking." Somehow she thought it might not be a good idea to tell Phyllis exactly what she had been talking about. Felicia didn't think Phyllis would understand.

"Talking?" Phyllis echoed. "Fern and her mother were there in the car, and they said you were giving him something, and he was yelling at you. What were you talking about?"

"Oh, we were just — talking."

"Really, Felicia," Phyllis began, sounding as if she were talking to a six-year-old, "you cause the worst traffic jam in the *entire* history of the school, and you were just — "

"Me?" Felicia said indignantly. "I was just trying to — "

"All right, people," Ms. De Mara said, coming back into the room, "we'll have to stop now."

But I was just trying to help, Felicia thought unhappily. I was just trying to give him a little constructive criticism. A little constructive criticism never hurt anyone.

Did it?

4

It had stopped raining when Felicia came home that afternoon.

Her first major project as a critic had apparently not turned out well at all. At lunch, Phyllis, Lorraine and Fern had practically cross-examined her about the traffic jam they said she had caused, and Felicia hadn't been able to say anything at all that even sounded believable to explain what she'd been doing.

They'd kept at her until Phyllis got tired of it, and began talking about clubs again. Felicia, relieved that they were finally letting her alone, had eaten her lunch without taking part in their conversation, or even listening to what they were saying.

"Where's Mom?" Felicia asked as Marilyn came into the kitchen with a bottle of shampoo, a bottle of cream rinse, a tube of hair conditioner and a bottle of setting gel.

"Upstairs," Marilyn replied, setting all her things on the counter next to the kitchen sink. "On the phone with Aunt Celeste."

"Oh," said Felicia, wrinkling up her nose. Aunt Celeste was kind of — well, Aunt Celeste was not one of Felicia's favorite people. She wasn't one of her *un*favorite people either, but she had the knack of making Felicia feel sort of ill at ease and childish whenever she was with her.

Felicia went to the refrigerator to get something to eat.

"See if there's a lemon in there, will you?" Marilyn said, her head under the faucet. "I'm going to rinse my hair three times and then use a lemon rinse after the cream rinse."

Felicia looked at the array of bottles and tubes already on the countertop.

"Aren't you afraid your hair will fall out with all that guck on it?" Felicia asked, fumbling around in the crisper for a lemon.

"What?" Marilyn asked from under the faucet. "I can't hear you."

"Never mind," Felicia muttered. She noticed the fatty pot roast her mother had complained about the day before, sitting in a ceramic bowl in some sort of purplish liquid. That must be the wine marinade her mother was making yesterday.

"The lemon!" Marilyn yelled. "Where's the lemon?"

"Here, here," Felicia said, sticking a lemon into Marilyn's groping hand.

"Now how am I supposed to — would you cut it, please, and squeeze it into a glass?"

"I'm not your slave," Felicia said irritably.

"Please, dearest sister, would you cut me a lemon and squeeze it into a glass, and I will be eternally grateful — "

"Oh, all right, all right," Felicia grumbled. "You don't have to be sarcastic."

She cut the lemon in half and squeezed it into a glass. She put the glass next to Marilyn, who still had her head in the sink.

Felicia opened the refrigerator again and stared at the pot roast. It certainly is fatty, she thought. Why didn't her mother take it back? How would they know that she was angry if she didn't tell them? Weren't you supposed to let a store know when you were dissatisfied? Stores were supposed to welcome constructive criticism.

Criticism, thought Felicia bitterly. Maybe I'd better forget about being a critic. I'm not too good at it after all. She remembered the traffic jam that morning and winced.

She closed the refrigerator door firmly.

On the other hand, Felicia thought, I did do a

good job on the broom closet. After all, one failure shouldn't stop anyone. And maybe, Felicia thought, it wasn't a failure. I mean, how could you tell? Maybe the timing hadn't been too good, but after all, the policeman hadn't even looked at the notes and diagram yet, so you really couldn't say she had failed.

She opened the refrigerator door again.

That really was a fatty pot roast. And packing it so you couldn't see the fat — that certainly seemed dishonest.

She took the bowl out of the refrigerator. She got a big plastic bag, and pulling the pot roast by the string, got it out of the marinade and into the bag.

"I'm going out for a while," she said to Marilyn, who was still leaning over the sink.

"I can't hear you!" Marilyn yelled.

"I'm going out!" Felicia repeated loudly.

"Good-bye!" Marilyn said.

When Felicia got to the store there were quite a few people at the meat counter and Felicia, remembering how traffic had gotten tied up that morning because of poor timing, waited for everybody else to talk to the butcher and leave. Even when it was finally Felicia's turn, another woman came up to the counter and Felicia told her to go first. She didn't want to feel like she was holding up a line of customers and causing a people-jam. She grinned to herself.

"I need some veal shanks," the woman said.

"How much, lady?"

"About five pounds."

"You'll have to wait," he said, going around into the back.

Felicia and the woman waited and waited. It seemed like forever. The woman kept looking at her watch and tapping her foot. She began to look at the meat in the cases, picking through steaks and roasts, and flinging the packages around as she rummaged through them.

Felicia was tired of waiting so long, and she was hungry. She hadn't eaten anything since lunch.

The butcher came back.

"That certainly took long enough," the woman snapped.

"We don't got veal shanks," he said shortly.

"You don't — " The woman stared at him angrily for a moment. Then she turned and stalked off.

The meat man looked down at the display case. The woman had certainly made a jumble out of it. The man looked suspiciously at Felicia, and back down at the mess.

He thinks I did it! Felicia realized suddenly. That'll

put him in a bad mood before I even say anything. There was no one else waiting. Now Felicia forgot she was tired of standing there, and wished there were a few more people ahead of her.

"I'd like to return this," Felicia said rapidly, holding out the plastic bag for him to see. "It's all fatty. You put the fat on the bottom so my mother — so no one could see it."

"Your mother send you?" he asked, pulling the plastic bag open.

"No," said Felicia.

"Hey, what is this? This meat is gray. What's the matter with you? I can't take this back."

"Why not?" Felicia asked. "I want a — a *refund*."

"You put something on it. I can't sell this."

He put it back in the bag and shoved it roughly at Felicia.

"But I don't want you to sell it," Felicia said reasonably. "That's just the point. It's all fatty. Why should someone else get stuck with it?"

"Stuck with it?" he growled. "It's perfectly good meat. It's a pot roast, it's supposed to have fat on it. There's nothing wrong with this meat. Or at least, there wasn't anything wrong with it before you put that stuff over it that made it turn gray."

"Are you the manager?" Felicia demanded boldly.

It seemed to her that if *she* knew about meat being marinated, a butcher should certainly know about it, and this man didn't seem to.

"I'm the assistant to the manager, and what I say goes. So beat it, kid. We're not taking that back. You don't even have a cash register receipt," he added.

How does he know, Felicia thought bitterly. I *might* have a receipt. But she didn't, and he'd already turned away from her and gone back through the swinging door.

Felicia walked dejectedly toward the front entrance of the store. She was angry and disappointed at the same time. He had been very rude. Now she had to carry the meat back home again and her mother would know she had failed.

"What you got there?"

Felicia looked up, startled. A man in a brown suit, carrying a clipboard and pen, was standing next to her.

"A pot roast," Felicia replied sourly. "A very fatty one, too."

"What are you doing with it?" he asked.

"I'm taking it back home. I was trying to return it, but — "

"Well, get it out of here," he ordered, walking away. "It's dripping."

Felicia looked down. The bag had somehow gotten a small hole in it, and it *was* dripping. She held it from the bottom, so the bag couldn't split and let the meat fall out, and hurried out of the store. Only then did she realize, with dismay, that the man had thought she might be stealing something.

Felicia could not remember when she had ever felt so insulted.

Felicia's father was home when she got back, and she heard her parents talking in the kitchen.

". . . gone!" her mother was saying. "Gone! I can't imagine what happened to it. Here's the bowl, here's the marinade, but the meat is *gone*."

Felicia would have liked to sneak into the kitchen and put the pot roast back into the bowl without anyone catching her, but she knew that was impossible. It sounded like her mother was going to stand there and stare at the empty bowl forever.

"Are you looking for this?" she asked gloomily, carrying the bag into the kitchen.

"Felicia!" her mother exclaimed. "What were you doing with my pot roast?"

"It's a long story," she said evasively.

"Oh, it's too late to make it now. It's got to simmer for at least three hours. But what were you *doing* with it?"

"Maybe they were using it for third base," her father suggested.

"That is not funny!" her mother snapped.

"Actually, I don't play much baseball," Felicia said, trying to change the subject.

"We'll go out to dinner," her father said. "You can make that tomorrow night."

"Felicia, I really want to know what you were doing with that pot roast," her mother persisted.

"I was going to return it," Felicia sighed. "Because it was so fatty. When are we going out to eat?"

"I guess as soon as Marilyn finishes drying her hair."

"Too bad," said Mr. Kershenbaum. "I was hoping to go tonight."

"Oh, it won't take her *that* long," grinned Mrs. Kershenbaum. "Felicia, I want to know — "

But Felicia had slipped out of the kitchen while she had the chance. She didn't want two cross-examinations in one day. Phyllis's had been enough.

Felicia didn't know whether she was angry or sad. It was a funny feeling, she thought, not knowing what you were feeling. She was angry because the assistant meat manager had been so nasty, but she was sad because she had failed to get him to take back the meat. She had pictured herself handing her mother the refund money, and her mother's surprised appre-

ciation: "Why, Felicia, how did you *ever* manage?"
"Oh," Felicia would have said, "I think the stores *welcome* a little constructive criticism."

But now — Felicia sighed. What hurt most, she decided, was being treated rudely because she was young. Maybe if she'd been her mother's age, the man would have listened. But because she wasn't, and didn't shop much in supermarkets, he figured she wasn't important enough to pay attention to.

That seemed pretty unfair. After all, you were entitled to make an honest complaint if you had one, and shouldn't they listen to you no matter how old or young you were? Just because you were young, didn't mean they could —

Felicia stopped on the stairs. She realized now that she was mostly angry, and anger made her determined to do something. She hadn't even spoken to the meat manager, just the assistant meat manager. Why should she give up so easily? She could write to the meat manager — no, the manager of the store, that would be even better! — and no one would know how old she was from a letter. She wasn't going to stop just because she had one setback.

In fact, now that she was so insulted and angry over the way she had been treated, she was going to try even harder to get her mother's money back. Why, she would write to the president of the supermarket chain himself if she had to!

Felicia went to the little table in the upstairs hall where her mother kept some stationery. It was engraved "Mrs. Arnold Kershenbaum" and was very important-looking. The only stationery Felicia had was a gift from her eighth birthday party. It had candy canes on it. She wanted this letter to look neat and businesslike.

She rummaged through her desk for a pen, but all she could find were pencils and crayons. She must have left all her pens in school.

"Marilyn," she said, going into her sister's room, "can I borrow a pen?"

"I can't hear you!" Marilyn screamed over the noise of her hair dryer.

"A pen!" Felicia screamed back. "I need a pen."

"Don't you have any pens?"

"If I had a pen," Felicia yelled, "would I ask you for one?"

"On the desk," Marilyn said, and went back to practicing a strange-looking, open-mouthed expression in the mirror as she dried her hair.

Marilyn had a shiny plastic pencil cup with black and white daisies on it, and Felicia fished out a ball-point pen from there. Looking down at Marilyn's desk, she noticed a piece of paper with her sister's handwriting on it. She saw, with bewilderment, that the paper read: "Marilynne. Marylin. Maralin. Maralyn. Marylinne. Marolin. Marolyn. Marolynne."

Felicia shrugged and turned away from the desk.

"Be sure and give it back!" her sister yelled. "Don't break it!"

Felicia looked down at the twenty-nine-cent pen.

"I won't break it," she assured her sister.

"What?" Marilyn shrieked.

"I won't break it!" Felicia yelled, her throat beginning to feel sore.

"And don't lose it!"

Felicia closed the door behind her and went into her own room.

She sat down at her desk and turned on the lamp. Maybe she ought to make a practice copy of the letter first, so she could decide what to say, and not have to cross anything out and make the letter look messy.

"Dear Sir or Madam:" Felicia began. That part was easy. They had learned how to write business letters in school. They had never learned how to do complaining letters, though; all their business letters seemed to be ordering things from companies, not trying to return things to companies.

I am writing to you because I am not satis-fied with one of your pot roasts which was bought at your store yesterday. I tried to return it today, and was spoken to very rudely by the man I spoke to at the meat counter. I am very angry because your pot roast was four pounds and there was at least one pound of fat on it.

This isn't hard at all, Felicia thought happily, writing quickly now. I really am good at complaining!

It wasn't until after seven o'clock that they drove into the parking lot of the Red Roof Restaurant. By this time, everybody, even Marilyn, who had held them all up waiting for her very long hair to dry, was starved.

"I hope the service is good," said Mr. Kershenbaum, as they sat down in one of the red plastic booths. "Everybody order something they can cook fast."

Felicia looked at her menu. She was so hungry that everything sounded mouth-watering. Should she get the fried jumbo shrimp or the chopped sirloin steak? Maybe hot turkey with gravy and sage dressing? Franks and beans with applesauce and sauerkraut? Felicia felt her stomach rumble.

"My sentiments exactly," her father said, grinning as she looked up to see if anyone had noticed.

"Chopped sirloin steak sounds good," Felicia said hesitantly.

"That's hamburger," her mother translated.

"Without a roll," her father added.

"Oh. Well, maybe the fried jumbo shrimp, with tartar sauce and french fries," Felicia read from the menu.

"That sounds good," her mother agreed. "I'll have that too."

Marilyn decided on the Dieter's Delite: cottage cheese with fresh fruit and a piece of Ry-Krisp. Her father wanted the turkey.

Their minds made up, they all sat back and waited for the waitress to come and take their order.

They waited.

"Where *is* she?" Felicia demanded, swiveling around in her seat.

"I may faint," Marilyn announced grimly.

Every time he caught a glimpse of the waitress who had brought them their water and menus, Mr. Kershenbaum signaled frantically at her, but she never seemed to be looking their way.

Finally she strolled over to their table, as if she had just now remembered them.

"You folks ready to order?" she asked, her pencil poised over her pad.

They gave her their orders.

Then they tried to wait patiently for their dinners to be served.

Felicia drank water.

Her mother played with the packets of sugar.

Her father drummed his fingers on the blue table top.

Felicia ran out of water.

"I *am* going to faint," Marilyn decided.

"Don't," her father warned. "I'm too weak to carry you out of here."

The waitress finally reappeared with their food.

"Sorry to keep you waiting," she said, not sounding very sorry at all. *She* wasn't starving, Felicia thought resentfully.

"Hey, where's my tartar sauce?" Felicia yelped as the waitress walked away.

"We're out of it," she called back over her shoulder.

"Rats!" Felicia grumbled. "That was the only reason I wanted the shrimp, so I could dip it in the tartar sauce."

"How's the turkey?" her mother asked her father.

"The turkey's okay," he gasped, grabbing for his

water glass, "but I think they dropped a whole box of pepper on the stuffing."

Felicia ate her shrimp without much enjoyment. It tasted flat without the tartar sauce.

"I think they fried this in bacon fat," her mother said, wrinkling up her nose.

"I don't know what you're all complaining about," Marilyn said. "Mine is fine."

"Sure," her father replied. "What can they do to cottage cheese?"

When they were finished they waited for the waitress to come back so they could order dessert and coffee. Felicia wanted peppermint ice cream.

"We don't have it today," the waitress said when she finally arrived. "How about pistachio?"

"I hate pistachio," Felicia said fervently. "It says on the menu you have thirty-eight flavors, including peppermint."

"Sorry," the waitress shrugged.

"Chocolate chip," Felicia said without enthusiasm.

The waitress looked delighted. "We got that," she nodded happily.

"This is a terrible place," Felicia whispered loudly after the waitress had brought their desserts and coffee. "Why did we come here?"

"Please, Felicia," her mother said tiredly, "let's not discuss it. We won't come again."

Felicia boiled inside. No tartar sauce, no peppermint ice cream, after waiting forever for your food, you didn't even enjoy it — this restaurant could sure use some constructive criticism!

And it'll get some constructive criticism, Felicia thought suddenly. The owner of the restaurant ought to know why I'll never come here again!

"Can I borrow a pencil?" Felicia asked her father.

"Will a pen do?" he asked, reaching into his breast pocket.

"What are you writing?" her mother asked as Felicia began to scribble on a paper napkin.

"Oh, just some stuff," she answered.

Service is slow, she was writing. *We had to wait too long for everything. You didn't have anything that I wanted. No tartar sauce. Too much pepper on the turkey stuffing. I ran out of water and no one gave me more. Cooked the shrimp in bad fat. No thirty-eight flavors.*

The waitress brought their check and Felicia folded up her napkin.

"This is for you," Felicia said to her. "It's a list of suggestions."

"Felicia!" her mother gasped.

"But you *said* we'd never come here again," Felicia protested. "I wanted them to know — "

"Felicia," her father threatened.

Marilyn slid out of the booth and hurried toward the front of the restaurant, pretending she didn't know her family at all.

"Suggestions?" the waitress repeated blankly, opening up the napkin.

Felicia's parents stood up. Her father grabbed her by the arm and hustled her to the cashier, who sat near the front entrance. He paid their bill quickly and they practically pushed Felicia out the door. Felicia looked back at the waitress. She was standing near their table, reading the list of criticisms with a sour expression on her face. A man two tables over was waving at her, trying to get her attention.

"Why did you do that?" her mother hissed at her when they were in the car.

"I was just giving a little constructive criticism," she defended herself.

"I was never so embarrassed in my *whole life*," Marilyn wailed.

"Why?" Felicia demanded. "Why is everyone so upset? All I did is tell them what we were thinking. We should complain if we pay money to go there and it's no good."

"Oh," her father groaned, "I forgot to leave a tip."

"A tip!" Felicia shrieked in outrage. "But she didn't *deserve* a tip!"

"Felicia!" her mother snapped.

Felicia slumped back in the seat.

"Well, she didn't," she murmured.

"I was *never* so embarrassed in my *life*," Marilyn insisted.

They pulled into the driveway.

"Where," Felicia's father asked suddenly, "is my pen?"

Felicia closed her eyes tightly. "I left it in the restaurant," she whispered.

"That was a brand-new pen," he said softly.

"Do you want to go back and get it?" Felicia asked.

"NO!" they yelled, in angry chorus.

Felicia had the uncomfortable feeling that they were all pretty annoyed with her. And she still didn't quite understand why.

5

"Felicia, please make your bed and straighten your room. Aunt Celeste and Uncle Henry will be here at two."

Felicia looked up from her reading.

"Okay," she said, only half listening.

"Oh," her mother noticed approvingly, "Aunt Celeste's new book."

"Yeah."

"Well, hurry up. I want this room clean before they get here."

"I'll be finished soon," Felicia said absently.

When her mother left the room, Felicia slipped her Criticism Notebook out from underneath Aunt Celeste's book. After the experience in the Red Roof Restaurant, she thought it might be better not to discuss her career as a constructive critic with her family.

In her Criticism Notebook Felicia was writing her thoughts about Aunt Celeste's newest book for children. Felicia's mother had said that there were critics of plays and movies and books; Felicia thought that maybe her problem as a constructive critic had been in criticizing *people*, like the waitress and the crossing guard. Maybe a constructive critic had to criticize *things*, like broom closets and books, and that way nobody's feelings would be hurt.

So Felicia was writing a review of Aunt Celeste's latest work, *Timmy and Tammy Visit a Solid Waste Recycling Plant*.

But even though she was criticizing a book instead of a person, Felicia did not think she would mention this to her mother. Her mother might get upset and worry that she might insult Aunt Celeste, or something.

Felicia sighed, and made a few more notes. Aunt Celeste had written a very dull book this time. It sounded like Felicia's old first grade reader: "Oh," said Timmy, "here we are at the solid waste recycling plant. Look, Tammy, look. What is that?"

Of course, maybe you had to be six to appreciate Aunt Celeste's book. After all, it wasn't written for kids of Felicia's age.

But did they have to talk like that, Timmy and Tammy? Felicia tried to remember when she was six, and she thought of all the six-year-olds she knew now, and she couldn't think of any six-year-old who talked like Timmy and Tammy, except in her first grade reader.

"Timmy and Tammy don't talk like real kids," she noted.

Felicia finished taking notes and began to write her review. Better hurry, she thought, with an anxious glance at the clock. She still had her room to clean and a list of suggestions she wanted to make for her cousin Marshall.

Felicia's pen scrawled feverishly across the paper. She wasn't even aware of the passing of time. She finished the book review, and was just about done with her list of suggestions for Marshall when her mother called her.

Already? Felicia thought, jumping up from her desk. The clock read ten of two. Time sure flies when you're concentrating, she observed to herself.

"Coming!" she called. She scooped the book review and her aunt's book off the desk and ran downstairs.

"Felicia!" cried Aunt Celeste, swooping her into her arms, "you're reading my book."

"She was reading it all morning," her mother said. "She was so absorbed I'm sure she forgot to clean her room." Felicia grinned sheepishly at her mother.

"Where's Marilyn?" Uncle Henry asked. "Still in hiding?"

Felicia's mother rolled her eyes at Uncle Henry and

made a funny little grimace with her mouth.

"Marilyn!" Uncle Henry boomed. "Come down and say hello!"

There was the sound of a door slamming upstairs, and then Marilyn came trudging down the stairs. She was wearing frayed jeans, a T-shirt with a picture of a buffalo on the front, and no shoes.

"Well, now," her uncle grinned, "you didn't have to get all dressed up for *us*."

"Marilyn, dear," Aunt Celeste cooed, hugging her.

"Hi," Marilyn said.

"Neat," said Marshall, pointing to Marilyn's bare feet. "Purple toenails."

"Come on, everyone," Felicia's father said, "coffee time. I made one of my famous Kershenbaum cakes for the occasion."

"Oh, how nice!" Aunt Celeste said eagerly. "What kind did you make this time?"

"He only knows how to make two kinds," Marilyn said.

"Chocolate layer," her father replied, glaring at Marilyn.

"My favorite," said Uncle Henry loyally.

After everyone had eaten the cake and Felicia and Marshall had finished their milk, Felicia's mother said, "Are you still taking piano lessons, Marshall?"

"Oh, yes," Aunt Celeste answered, before her son could say anything, "you don't just let a talent like Marshall's lie *fallow*, you know. It would be a crime."

"Why don't you play something for us?" Felicia's mother suggested.

Marshall looked at Felicia and made a face like he was going to throw up.

"Yes, dear. Why don't you?" his mother urged.

Felicia smiled sympathetically at her cousin and shrugged.

"Do I have to?" Marshall asked dully.

"Why, no, Marshall," Aunt Celeste said carefully, "you don't *have* to if you don't want to; although we'll all be *very* disappointed if you — "

"Aw, the hell with it," Marshall mumbled, and clumped over to the piano.

"Marshall, play 'Waltz of the Flowers,'" Aunt Celeste said. "Oh, he plays this so beautifully; wait till you hear. Go on, Marshall."

"He knows it by heart?" Felicia's father asked.

"Perfectly," Aunt Celeste nodded, "just listen. Go on, Marshall, we're all ears."

Marshall began to play.

Aunt Celeste looked from Marshall to Felicia's parents to see their reaction, and then back to Marshall, as if she couldn't bear to take her eyes off him for more than a second.

Felicia winced as her cousin played three wrong notes in a row.

Marshall played an A flat that sounded sick, forgot where he was, and had to go back to the beginning. He became angry, and the angrier he got, the louder he played. As his fingers crashed out chords they slipped, and he made more mistakes. Aunt Celeste bit her lip.

Marilyn sighed deeply and slumped in her chair. Uncle Henry toyed with a cigar band. Felicia's mother smiled wanly.

Felicia realized that Marshall really needed that list of suggestions she had for him up in her room.

"That was very nice, Marshall," Felicia's mother said, clapping weakly when Marshall had finished playing and slammed the piano lid down.

"It stunk," Marshall muttered.

"I don't understand it," fretted Aunt Celeste, "he plays it perfectly at home, absolutely perfectly from beginning to end without *one mistake*."

"I do not," Marshall said disgustedly.

"Marshall, why don't you and Felicia go downstairs and play Ping-Pong?" her father suggested.

"You want to?" Felicia asked her cousin.

"Okay."

"Listen, Marshall," Felicia said a little later, while they were trying to retrieve one of Marshall's smashes from behind the dryer, "did it ever occur to you that the piano might not be the best thing for you to play?"

"Are you kidding? My *mother* is the only one who it never occurred to."

"Come on up to my room," Felicia said, putting down her paddle. "I want to show you something."

They ran up the stairs.

"Where's the fire?" Uncle Henry asked as they raced through the dining room.

"Now look, I made a list for you," Felicia began when they were in her room with the door closed.

"A list?" repeated Marshall curiously. "What kind of a list?"

"It's a list of instruments besides the piano that you could try," she explained.

"Let me see," Marshall said, taking the list from her.

"Hey, this is something," he commented. "You really went to a lot of trouble. Bongo drums, vibraphone, banjo, glockenspiel — what's a glockenspiel?"

"It's like a xylophone. They play it in marching bands," Felicia explained.

"Mandolin, harmonica, guitar — *that's* what I really want to play," Marshall said longingly, "the guitar."

"Well then, why don't you?"

"You know why I don't," Marshall replied glumly.

"It was nice of you to go to all this trouble for me — I mean, don't think I don't appreciate it, and everything, but — "

"Look," Felicia said reasonably, "did you ever try to talk to your mother about the piano lessons?"

"Sure, plenty of times. Believe me, I've tried everything. I even went on a hunger strike once, but I had to practice anyway. She thinks I've got this great talent."

"Yeah, I know," Felicia nodded sympathetically.

"But I don't," Marshall groaned.

"Well, not on the piano, anyhow," Felicia agreed.

"So what's the use?" Marshall folded up the list into a tiny square, so small that he couldn't fold it any more. Then, thoughtfully, he began to unfold it.

"You know," he said slowly, "I never told her I'd be willing to play another instrument. I just told her I didn't want to play the piano." He smoothed out the list between his fingers.

"Maybe that's it," Felicia said excitedly. "Maybe she thinks if you don't play the piano you won't play anything, and that would let your talent lie *fallow*." Whatever that means, Felicia thought suddenly.

"But if we *compromise*," Marshall went on, "you know, like I'd go to all my guitar lessons, and practice without complaining, if she just lets me play what — "

"Felicia!"

From downstairs her mother's angry voice reached them, even though the door was closed.

"Uh oh," Marshall said, "she sure sounds mad."

"She sure does," Felicia agreed nervously.

"Felicia, *come down here!*"

They looked at each other and Marshall shrugged. Felicia opened the door and her cousin followed her to the top of the stairs.

"What?" Felicia asked.

"I asked you to come here!"

"Oh, Rosalind," they heard Aunt Celeste saying, "please don't make such a fuss. It's funny, really it is." But Aunt Celeste didn't really sound like she thought it was funny, whatever "it" was.

Felicia walked slowly down the steps, with Marshall so close behind her he scraped her heels twice.

"What is this?" her mother demanded, waving a piece of paper at her.

" I don't know," Felicia said, puzzled. "Let me see."

Her mother thrust the paper at her.

"Oh," Felicia brightened, "it's my review of Aunt Celeste's book." She looked at her mother's stormy face and felt her stomach plunge.

"But you said that critics write about books," she began miserably, "and I thought — "

"Now, Rosalind," Aunt Celeste said soothingly, "please, it's ridiculous to get so angry at her. She was just doing a book report, really, like she does in school, only she was doing it on *my* book."

"Celeste," Felicia's mother said, "she has got to learn that other people have feelings besides her, and — "

"Well, I have feelings, Rosalind," Aunt Celeste persisted, "and I feel very badly that I'm the reason you're angry with Felicia. So please, if you care about how *I* feel, let's forget the whole thing."

Felicia looked down at the floor. She couldn't bear the threatening silence as they waited for her mother's response. She could sense the embarrassment in the room, almost like a smell, and she felt the awful uncomfortableness of being to blame.

But still, she thought, when we talked about being a critic, *she* thought it was a good idea. *She* said I very well might be a critic some day. She didn't say, only tell the truth if it's nice. Why did she let me go ahead, if she doesn't really want me to? Felicia fought back tears of anger and embarrassment.

"All right," Felicia's mother said grimly, "forget it." But she didn't sound like she was going to forget it very quickly.

"Now, dear," Aunt Celeste said briskly, taking

Felicia's arm and leading her over to the couch, "tell me what it was that you thought was wrong with the book."

Felicia gaped at Aunt Celeste.

"But —"

Her mother threw up her arms in despair and stalked into the kitchen.

"Encourage her, why don't you," remarked Marilyn.

Uncle Henry tried to suppress a grin.

"Now, here you say, 'Timmy and Tammy don't sound real.' What did you mean by that?"

Felicia beamed. Why, Aunt Celeste wasn't mad at all! She wanted Felicia's opinion about her book! It was just her mother who was embarrassed, and there wasn't even any reason to be! Felicia settled happily on the couch next to Aunt Celeste.

"Well, I thought they didn't talk like real children," she explained seriously.

"They don't?" Aunt Celeste said, raising her eyebrow.

"No, I don't think so," Felicia said, opening the book. "Like here, listen: 'Oh, oh, look, look! What is that big machine? What is that big machine doing? What is it? What is it?'"

"Of course, you understand, dear," Aunt Celeste

began with a pained smile, "this book is written for children much younger than *you*. They don't read as well as *you* do yet, so perhaps that's why the language seems a little — simple to you."

"Well, I don't know," Felicia said doubtfully, "I don't think you have to — "

"Felicia," her father said warningly, looking up from the chess game he was playing with Marshall.

"No, no, Arnold," Aunt Celeste protested, "the *child* is entitled to her opinion and we must respect it."

"Who must?" said Marilyn disgustedly.

"Help me in the kitchen, Marilyn!" her mother shouted.

"Now go on, dear," ordered Aunt Celeste.

"Well, I was just thinking," Felicia said, "that you could make it easy to read without making them not sound like real children. You know, maybe if they didn't say everything twice; 'oh, oh, look, look.' "

"I see," said Aunt Celeste, her lips in a thin little line.

"And real kids don't say — "

"DINNER'S READY!" Felicia's mother yelled from the kitchen.

"Well!" her father said heartily, jumping up from the chess board, "Let's go, everyone; I'm starved.

Come on, Celeste, come on, Henry, food time!"

"Checkmate," Marshall said quietly, grinning up at his uncle.

"What do you know, Celeste, he won again!" Felicia's father said merrily.

Felicia looked at him, puzzled. Her father hated to lose to Marshall, and usually when he did, he scowled and frowned, and accused everyone of jabbering so much he couldn't concentrate. Now he was sounding practically cheerful about losing.

Felicia shook her head in confusion. Everybody was certainly acting strange this afternoon.

Aunt Celeste folded Felicia's review carefully in half and placed it in her pocketbook.

"What's for dinner?" Uncle Henry asked hungrily.

"Leg of lamb," said Felicia's mother.

Felicia and Marshall looked at each other and wrinkled up their noses.

"My favorite!" exclaimed Uncle Henry, Aunt Celeste and Felicia's father, all at once.

Felicia couldn't understand why her father acted so surprised. He knew they were having leg of lamb, didn't he?

6

". . . and the current temperature is forty-three W G V M degrees."

"Forty-five," said Felicia automatically, glancing out the window at the thermometer.

"Arrggghh!" Marilyn shrieked.

"You know, that really annoys me," Felicia said irritably. "They *never* get it right."

"Tell them," Marilyn urged hoarsely. "Tell them — but for God's sake, stop telling *us*."

"I will!" said Felicia suddenly. "Now why didn't I think of it before?" She hurried to the phone and dialed Information.

"What is she doing?" demanded Marilyn.

"She's using the phone," her father replied, and winced as Marilyn scowled at him.

"Are you calling the radio station?" her mother asked as Felicia hung up the phone and started to dial again.

"Sure," Felicia said brightly. "*Somebody* ought to tell them."

"And of course," her mother said drily, "that somebody has to be you."

"No doubt they'll be thrilled to hear from her," Marilyn predicted.

"Shh!" hissed Felicia waving her hand at Marilyn.

"Hello, my name is Felicia Kershenbaum and I — Felicia . . . Kershenbaum . . . K-E-R- that's right. . . . Well, I was listening to your weather report and you gave the wrong temperature. . . . Well, because my thermometer says forty-five, and you said it was forty-three. . . . Sure, I'm sure. . . . Well, because it's a very accurate thermometer. . . . Uh huh. . . . Plainville. . . . Yes, but you always give the wrong — uh huh. . . . Okay. . . . Okay, good-bye."

Felicia hung up.

"That was Ray Raymond himself, I talked to!" Felicia said excitedly.

"Isn't he on the air now?" her mother asked.

"He was playing a record," Felicia explained, "but he said he was going to — shh! Listen!"

The record stopped, and the voice on the radio said, "And we had a call from Felicia Kershenbaum — "

Felicia's stomach felt skittery as she heard her name announced over the air.

"She says the temperature we gave was wrong; Felicia's thermometer reads forty-five degrees. Well,

Felicia, maybe it's two degrees warmer where you live, but our superaccurate W G V M meteorological equipment tells us that the temperature outside our W G V M studios is forty-three."

Felicia slumped in her chair. They didn't believe her! Ray Raymond had said he'd give her temperature reading over the air, and it sounded like he was practically laughing at her!

"Oh God," Marilyn moaned, "I will die of embarrassment."

"Why?" her father asked innocently. "What's embarrassing?"

"They said her *name* on the *air!*" Marilyn wailed. "That's *my* name too, you know!"

"For heaven's sake, Marilyn," her mother said impatiently, "they didn't announce her name on the air because she was arrested for murder."

"No, they announced her name on the air because she's Pest of the Year, that's why!" Marilyn raged. "And because she's a dope, and always has to —"

Felicia cringed under Marilyn's storm of words.

"That's enough, Marilyn," her mother said coldly. "There's no need to carry on like that. It's my name too, and I'm not embarrassed."

"Shh, listen!" Their father turned up the radio.

". . . and those five people who called us," Ray

Raymond was saying, "all agreed with Felicia that indeed, in Plainville, it is definitely forty-five degrees. So, Felicia, it looks like you were right, after all, and your thermometer is as reliable for Plainville as ours is right outside our W G V M studios, where it is now forty-two W G V M degrees."

"Forty-three," Felicia said, glancing out the window.

"Yow!" Marilyn screamed, and lunged from her chair and out of the room.

"I heard your name on the radio this morning," Cheryl said as they came into the classroom.

"So did I," said Phyllis, who came in right behind them. "That was just like you, Felicia."

Just like you! What did that mean? Felicia frowned. Was there something wrong about being right? Felicia had never had her name on the radio before, so how was it "just like her" to be announced on Ray Raymond's program?

Felicia took her seat, noticing that Phyllis and Cheryl had their heads close together at Cheryl's desk, whispering about something. Felicia gazed down at her looseleaf notebook, rubbing the vinyl cover with her finger. There was a funny sort of emptiness in her stomach. She wondered what they were talking about. She glanced over at them. They looked like best friends telling each other deep secrets. Phyllis glanced at Felicia, then quickly back to Cheryl.

Were they talking about her, Felicia wondered miserably? Was Cheryl suddenly so friendly with Phyllis that she didn't care that Felicia was sitting alone while they discussed her?

Felicia slipped her math homework out of her notebook and sighed. They hadn't even said the Pledge of Allegiance yet, and she wished it were time to go home.

"Come on, Felicia," Cheryl said as they got their milk, "there's Phyllis and Lorraine."

Felicia's pleasure at going to the lunchroom with Cheryl evaporated.

"There's some seats over there," she said hopefully, pointing to another table.

"Don't be that way," Cheryl said impatiently, "they're saving a seat for me."

For you, Felicia thought unhappily. Saving a seat, but just for you.

Cheryl seemed to sense Felicia's thoughts and said, "For you too, silly. Come on."

Phyllis, Lorraine and Fern did most of the talking at lunch. From the corner of her eye, Felicia caught Cheryl glancing at her a couple of times, and frowning.

"I had an idea for a name," Lorraine said eagerly. "How about 'JABOGS'?"

"JABOGS?" Phyllis repeated, twisting her mouth around the word.

"Sure," Lorraine said. "It stands for 'Just A Bunch Of Girls.'"

"Blecch," Fern decided, making a face.

"What's wrong with it?" Lorraine demanded hotly. "I think it's cute."

"I don't know," Phyllis said doubtfully. "What do you think, Cheryl?"

Felicia stared at Cheryl, who looked sort of embarrassed. For the first time Felicia was paying attention to the conversation, and she realized that they were talking about a club of their own, and that Cheryl was going to be a member.

How could she do it? Felicia groaned inwardly. I wouldn't join *any* club if they didn't want my best friend.

"I don't know," Cheryl mumbled, avoiding Felicia's gaze.

"Now I was thinking," Phyllis went on, "of something like 'Daughters of Athena.'"

"Daughters of *Athena!*" Lorraine shrieked. "Are you kidding, Phyllis?"

"No, I am not kidding," Phyllis said coldly. "Athena was the goddess of wisdom, you know."

"Oh, brother," Lorraine jeered, "Daughters of Athena!"

"Have you a better suggestion?" Phyllis demanded.

"Sure, I told you. JABOGS."

"I said a *better* suggestion."

"Anything's better than Daughters of Athena, if you ask me," Lorraine said nastily.

The bell rang.

"Listen, Felicia," Cheryl whispered as they threw away their milk cartons and empty lunch bags, "don't worry about the club. They'll ask you to join."

"I'm not worried," Felicia said, blinking her eyes hard to hold back the tears. She discarded her half-eaten lunch.

"It doesn't matter if they don't want me in their old club. But," she said loyally, "if they asked me to join and not you, I never would."

"Well, neither would I!" Cheryl said indignantly. "You wait and see. You'll be in the club."

Felicia looked at her friend. "You really wouldn't join if they don't ask me too?"

"Of course not," Cheryl assured her. "You're my best friend, aren't you?"

Felicia felt so relieved she wanted to cry all over again. Until Cheryl had said so, Felicia had been not at all sure she still had a best friend.

As she left school in the afternoon, Felicia noticed that the crossing guard seemed to be doing something different. Felicia wondered what it was, and why she even noticed it, and then she realized.

He was following some of her suggestions! He had actually read her list of criticisms (*constructive* criticisms) and was using some of her ideas!

Felicia smiled broadly at him as she crossed the street.

He just nodded and said, "Move along," as if he didn't recognize her. But Felicia was sure he remembered her, even if he pretended not to. He probably just didn't want to say "Thank you" in front of all the other kids.

It was a good thing Marilyn wasn't home yet, Felicia thought to herself. She'd taken an apple and a package of peanut-butter-cheese crackers up to her room, and noticed that she still had Marilyn's pen on her desk. Now she could get it back to her sister's room before Marilyn had one of her screaming fits.

Felicia's mother was talking on her bedroom phone and hadn't even heard her come in. The day after Aunt Celeste and Uncle Henry had visited, she'd been very touchy, and snapped at Felicia a great deal, but she'd never come right out and said anything about why she was angry. By now she had gotten over it, Felicia supposed, because her mother had been her usual self for the past few days.

Felicia put Marilyn's pen into the pencil holder on her desk. That piece of paper with all the "Marilyns" spelled in all different ways was stuck under the pencil can. Suddenly, Felicia realized what her sister had been doing.

She'd been trying to find a new way to spell her name, because she didn't like it.

Felicia felt a sharp wave of sympathy for her sister. It must be terrible not to like your name! And a name like Marilyn — well, no matter how you spelled it, it was still Marilyn.

How else could you spell Felicia, she wondered, wandering back to her room and sitting down at her own desk again.

Felitia

Faleesha (yucchh)

Falisha

Well, it didn't matter, she thought, because Felicia was a nice name, just the way it was. It had a nice, soft sound. Marilyn, on the other hand . . .

A new name, Felicia thought suddenly. That's what Marilyn needs. With a new name, she'd be a new person, and maybe she wouldn't be so touchy all the time.

Now, what would be a good name?

Felicia tapped the end of the pencil against her teeth thoughtfully.

Augustina. That's nice. She wrote it down on her "From the desk of Felicia Kershenbaum" memo pad.

Laura. She wrote Laura on the pad.

Penelope. Very elegant, Felicia thought, and dignified. Marilyn would like that. And Penny is a nice nickname. For when she feels friendly.

Estrellita. Oh, that's beautiful, thought Felicia. It sounded exotic and romantic. She wondered where she had ever heard the name, but couldn't remember. Estrellita went on the list too.

Then Felicia ran out of ideas. She remembered that in the big dictionary they had in the den, there was a special section in the back with a list of first names. She ran to get it.

It was just what she needed. Felicia started reading down the alphabetical list and couldn't write fast enough to put down all the beautiful names she found.

Andriette. Angelica. Aurora. Belinda. Camilla. Cassandra. Cecily. Chloette. Christabel. Clarissa. Consuela. Delphine. Desiree. Esmeralda. Euphemia. Faustina. Fleurette . . .

"Marilyn," Felicia said, knocking on her sister's door later, "I want to show you something."

"What is it?"

Felicia opened the door and went in.

"The other day I noticed you were writing your name all different ways — "

"Snooping again!" Marilyn shrieked. "Can't I have *any* privacy in this house? Can't you keep out of my things? I don't go sneaking around in *your* room spying on *you*, do I?"

"Listen, Marilyn," Felicia protested, "the paper was right on your desk when I borrowed your pen. I couldn't help — "

"My pen!" Marilyn remembered. "Where's my pen?"

"Right back where you had it," Felicia said virtuously. "I didn't forget to give it back."

She handed Marilyn her list of names. "Anyway, I made this list for you. I thought you might pick a name you liked better than Marilyn."

"Who asked you?" Marilyn replied nastily. "I don't recall coming to you for suggestions."

"I just thought — "

"And that paper was my own personal private business!" she yelled. "You had no right spying on me!"

"I'm sorry," Felicia said meekly. "I didn't mean — "

"Oh, get out of here!" Marilyn snarled.

Felicia dropped her list of names on Marilyn's bed and fled from the room.

"I don't understand it," Felicia's mother said. "It's the strangest thing."

"What?" asked Felicia, wandering into the kitchen where her parents were talking.

"I got a letter and a check for ten dollars from the manager of Shopwise."

"Well, what did the letter say?" her father asked.

"They said they were giving me a refund for the pot roast that I was dissatisfied with," her mother said.

"Well, that's nice."

"But I never wrote to them about it," she said confusedly. "It's as if they read my mind. And they apologize for the discourtesy of the assistant meat department manager, and promise it won't happen again. Whatever that means."

"I wrote to them," Felicia announced. The moment

she had pictured in her mind had come after all!

"You!"

"That day when the pot roast was gone," Felicia explained. "I tried to take it back for you, and they wouldn't, and the man was so mean, I got mad and I wrote to the manager of the store. I gave him some constructive criticism."

"Isn't that something?" her father marveled. "You see, it pays to criticize when you're not — "

"Arnold, please," her mother said, glaring at him.

"Aren't you glad?" Felicia asked.

"Of course I am," her mother grinned, and Felicia felt relieved. "I think it was very clever of you. But I don't understand why they sent the letter to me, instead of you."

"Maybe because I used your stationery," Felicia suggested. "I guess they thought I was Mrs. Arnold Kershenbaum."

"Ohh," her mother breathed, finally understanding it all.

Marilyn came downstairs very slowly, head held high.

"Come on, Marilyn," her mother said, "it's just about time for dinner."

"My name," said Marilyn, with great dignity, "is no longer Marilyn."

"It isn't?" her father asked, startled.

"No," she said. "It is Desiree."

"Desiree?" her mother repeated unbelievingly.

"Yes. Desiree."

Felicia sighed happily. She *had* helped her sister after all. Marilyn — that is, Desiree — had liked her suggestion!

"Desiree?" her father mused. *"Desiree Kershenbaum?"*

7

"I am not going!" Marilyn proclaimed loudly. "I will not be humiliated —"

"Marilyn," her mother began wearily.

"*Desiree*," she corrected. "I wish you'd try and remember."

"We have to leave in an hour Mar — I mean, Dear," her mother coaxed.

"I am not a child," Marilyn said firmly. "I do not care to sit with *children*."

Felicia could hear the conversation in the bathroom, where she was sitting in a tub filled with Marilyn-Desiree's "Bubbles de Bain," getting clean and smelling deliciously of lilies of the valley. Her mother had put her hair up in big rollers, and she was being very careful to wash her neck without getting her hair wet.

"But, *Desiree*," her mother pleaded, "they just *call* it a children's table. All your cousins are sitting there. It's not only for little children."

"Felicia is a child," Marilyn said stubbornly. "I am not a child."

"You're not even listening to what I'm saying!" her mother cried.

Felicia heard the door slam, then a few minutes later, the sound of someone pounding on it."

"Marilyn!" her father called.

"Desiree!" came Marilyn's muffled voice.

"Get dressed, Marilyn!"

"I'm not sitting at the — "

"Marilyn, I don't care if you sit on top of the wedding cake, just cut out this nonsense and get dressed!"

Felicia heard drawers yanked open and slammed shut, and Marilyn-Desiree stomping around in her room, talking to herself, loud enough for Felicia to hear the muttering, but not loud enough to understand what she was saying.

Felicia dried herself off and dusted herself with clouds of Jasmine Bouquet talcum powder. She slipped on her bathrobe over her underwear and ran into her parents' bedroom.

"Will you do my hair now?" she asked her mother, hopping eagerly from one foot to the other.

"Oh, Felicia," her mother said, "I was just going to do my own."

"Please," Felicia begged, "I can't wait to see how it looks."

"All right, all right," her mother gave in.

She took all the rollers out of Felicia's hair and began to brush it, smoothing the waves with her hand as she stroked the brush firmly down the length of the hair.

Felicia sat in front of her mother's mirror and watched as her hair began to make a soft, sleek frame around her face. Her mother pulled the hair back from Felicia's forehead and slipped a green velvet band over her head.

"I look beautiful," Felicia breathed, when her mother stood back to survey her in the mirror.

"You look just like Alice in Wonderland," her father said, coming into the room.

"Now, hurry and get dressed," her mother said, giving her a little pat on the shoulder, "and let me get ready too. We have to be out of here in half an hour."

"Okay." Felicia jumped up.

"Oh," she said, looking at herself in the mirror one last time, "I really look beautiful."

"And you know what?" she remembered, pausing at the doorway. "I'm *so clean* — I even washed behind my knees!"

"Imagine that," her father marveled.

Felicia stepped into her dress so she wouldn't mess up her hair, and zipped it up in the back as far as she could. She put on her black patent leather shoes with the *heels* — they were tiny, fat heels, it was true, but they *were* heels — over her white stockings.

"Desiree," she said, running into her sister's room, "would you zip me?"

"Can't you learn to knock?" her sister snapped.

"I'm sorry," Felicia said cheerfully. Even Marilyn's nastiness could not spoil her mood.

Marilyn zipped her up in the back. Felicia started to turn so she could see herself in the full length mirror.

"Wait," Marilyn said, "there's a little hook in the back — there."

"Thank you."

"You look nice," Marilyn said grudgingly.

"Thanks," said Felicia with surprise. "So do you."

Marilyn was wearing a black dress with bunches of bright red cherries all over it. Felicia wasn't sure she liked it too much, but she couldn't criticize her sister just when she was being so nice — even if she would have looked better in something else.

Felicia looked at herself in the mirror. Her dress was deep green velvet, with a white crocheted collar and cuffs.

She thought she'd never looked so pretty in her life.

"I love weddings!" she said excitedly. "Don't you?"

Marilyn shrugged. "Eh."

"Are you girls ready?" their father called.

"Almost," Marilyn said. She applied mascara and eyeliner, brushed some red stuff on her cheeks that made them look pink, and then applied a lipstick that didn't make her lips any color at all, but made them look very wet. Felicia watched, fascinated, as her sister did all this.

"Would you put some of that on me?" Felicia asked timidly.

"Sure," said Marilyn, surprisingly agreeable.

"This is lip gloss — see, no color, just shine." Marilyn applied it carefully.

"Feels funny," Felicia said, rolling her tongue gently over her lips.

"Don't lick it off," Marilyn warned.

"Now, this is blusher," she explained, brushing just a tiny bit on each of Felicia's cheeks. "It gives you a healthy, natural glow."

Felicia looked in the mirror again. She didn't look too different, which was just as well, since she didn't think her mother would want her to look too different, but she *felt* beautiful.

"Are you *coming*?" their father demanded loudly.

"Yes, yes," Marilyn called. She grabbed her suede fringed shoulder bag and flung open her door.

"Well, you both look lovely," their father said. "It was almost worth waiting for you."

"You look very nice, Mar — Desiree," her mother said. "But, you're not taking that bag, are you?"

"It's the only one I've got," Marilyn reminded her.

"Oh, dear, maybe you'd better use one of mine," she said, hurrying into her room.

"Rosalind, it is four twenty-nine. We have to be out of here in exactly *one minute.*"

"We won't miss the wedding, will we?" Felicia fretted.

"They're not going to hold up the ceremony for us," her father replied darkly.

"Oh, Arnold, stop worrying the child!" her mother said. "No, we won't miss the wedding. We're all set. See, that didn't even take a minute."

She looked at Felicia critically. "What is that you've got on your lips?"

"Lip gloss," said Marilyn.

"Wipe it off," her mother ordered, handing Felicia a tissue.

"Oh, no!" she wailed. "Why? It isn't red or anything."

"It makes your lips kissably moist," Marilyn said.

"Just what she needs," her mother retorted.

"It also helps prevent chapped lips," Marilyn added.

Felicia looked gratefully at her sister, who was suddenly, and for once, sticking up for her.

"Come *on*," their father commanded, taking their mother's arm and leading them all downstairs.

Felicia licked her shiny lips contentedly.

The Lagoon Room of Trader Phil's Shangri-La, where the cocktail hour before the wedding ceremony and the dinner afterwards were to be held, was big enough so that even with all those people milling around, it wasn't crowded.

Felicia stared in awe at the fishnets hanging from the walls and ceilings, some with mermaids lounging in them (fake, Felicia assured herself), the dolphin fountain which spouted pink punch, and the palm trees (fake again, Felicia noted, feeling the plastic bark), around which some of Felicia's cousins were dizzily chasing each other.

The waiters, passing around the room with hot and cold cocktail snacks, wore some kind of funny, wraparound skirt, no shirts, and leis around their necks. Felicia giggled as she snatched a tiny frankfurter from a passing waiter who, along with his skirt and his flower necklace, wore aviator glasses, long, stringy blond hair, and basketball sneakers.

Felicia and her sister, firmly gripped by their mother's hands, had been introduced to a succession of distant relatives, friends of the bride and groom, and the bride's family.

Every time Felicia's mother said, "And this is my daughter *Marilyn*," Marilyn-Desiree scowled fiercely, and mumbled as she shook hands.

Felicia was kissed by Aunt Celeste, Aunt Sophy, Aunt Alma, Aunt Edna, and several people who remembered her from when she was a tiny baby, "no bigger than *that*," and whom she didn't remember at all.

By the time she found her cousins Marshall and Joyce, she was covered with lipstick, and thought she probably didn't need Marilyn's blusher in the first place, since she now had more color on her cheeks than her aunts could still have left on their lips.

Marshall and Joyce were standing next to the table with the dolphin fountain on it, and their faces were lipsticky too. Marshall had three empty paper cups next to his elbow, and was filling up a fourth. Joyce was rubbing fitfully at her cheeks.

"Try the punch," Marshall said to Felicia. "It's not bad."

"That's a darling dress," Joyce said coolly. Joyce was

only a year older than Felicia, but acted as if she were years more grown-up.

"Thanks," said Felicia, trying to get a glass of punch as the dolphin spurted it out in an arc and into the huge crystal bowl, on which he balanced on the tip of his tail.

"Use that big spoon if you're having trouble," Marshall advised, catching a cascade of punch in his cup with a practiced air.

Felicia did, and it was far easier to fill her cup with the ladle than the way Marshall was doing it.

She tasted it. It tasted funny.

Marshall plucked four miniature eggrolls off a passing waiter's tray.

Felicia's six-year-old twin cousins, Lance and Vance, tried to climb a palm tree and knocked it over.

Felicia's five-year-old cousin Michelle, who happened to be wearing her tap shoes, did a little dance for a circle of admiring aunts. When they clapped she curtseyed prettily. Then she began to go around the room to other people, tugging at their arms and asking them if they wanted to see her dance.

Felicia hardly had time to try any of the delicious-looking things laid out on the big table, when her mother found her, swooped her and Marshall and Joyce away from the food, and said, "Come on, the wedding's going to start!"

"But I haven't had anything hardly to eat!" Felicia objected.

"There'll be plenty to eat afterwards," her mother assured her.

"But this is the best part!" Felicia cried.

Marshall grabbed a napkin and began to throw things into it — tiny frankfurters, potato puffs, eggrolls, things on toothpicks and things on little circles of bread. He rolled up the ends of the napkin and stuffed it into his jacket pocket.

Felicia's mother didn't say anything, but she looked at Marshall disapprovingly.

"Really, Marshall," Joyce said, condescendingly.

The wedding ceremony was in a chapel right near the Lagoon Room, so they only had to walk down a large open hall to get to it. Felicia sat between Marshall and Joyce. Her mother didn't notice as Marshall slipped her eggrolls, hot dogs and canapes during the ceremony.

Felicia thought that she would be very moved by the wedding. She had hoped she would cry a little, since that's what people were supposed to do at weddings. But she couldn't hear too well, and she couldn't see too well, and she didn't even realize the exact moment when her cousin Josh and his bride were officially married, until there was a happy buzzing from the rest of the guests and the music started again, triumphantly, and Josh and Barbara hurried up the center aisle, smiling. Then Felicia felt a tightness in her throat, and a little thrill went through her at the sound of the joyful music.

After they stopped to shake hands at the receiving line, she and Marshall followed the rest of the people back to the Lagoon Room. While they had been watching the wedding, it had been miraculously transformed into a dining room. Tables were set with white cloths and sea green napkins, bowls of flowers and ferns.

"You're at Table Twenty-Seven," said Felicia's mother, coming up behind her. "We're at Table Fourteen, right over there," she pointed. "Where's Marilyn?"

"There she is," Marshall said. Marilyn was talking with a tall boy in a formal jacket who had been one of the ushers in the wedding party.

He waved as he went off to sit at the head table, and Marilyn slouched over to her mother.

"*He's* not sitting at the children's table," Marilyn said darkly.

"He's part of the wedding party," her mother tried to explain. "He has to sit at the head table. You didn't expect to sit with the bride and — "

But Marilyn walked off.

"You're at Table Twenty-Seven!" her mother called after her.

"Yippee," said Marilyn bleakly, over her shoulder.

Felicia and Marshall found that their table was right next to the band, which had begun to play as the people strolled into the Lagoon Room.

The band was very loud.

Felicia could hardly hear Marshall, even when he was practically shouting in her ear.

"Guess what?" he yelled.

"What?" Felicia yelled back.

"I'm taking guitar lessons!"

"That's great!"

"I did what you said," he shouted. "I told my mother I'd practice all the time without complaining if I could just play the instrument I wanted, and she finally said okay!"

"That's really good," Felicia said warmly.

"So thanks!" Marshall roared. "It was your idea!"

The band struck up "Here Comes the Bride" and Josh and Barbara entered the room, grinning nervously as they made their way to the head table.

Everybody applauded, and the accordion player began to sing, "The Way You Look Tonight." Barbara blushed a little. Marshall, who was sitting right under the accordion player, near the raised platform on which the band played, puffed out his cheeks and covered his mouth with his hand. The accordion player was not much of a singer.

There were little menu cards written in French. Everybody started eating their *Mélange des Fruits Suprême*, which was cut-up grapefruit and orange sections with a cherry half on top.

"What's *Potage des Légumes?*" Felicia asked Marshall.

"Pea soup!" Marshall howled, as the waiter, now dressed in regular waiter clothes, put a bowl down in front of him.

"Lentil soup," the waiter corrected him sternly.

Marshall tasted it and made a face. "Same thing," he proclaimed disgustedly.

Joyce was sitting on the other side of Felicia, talking to Marilyn. When the band occasionally stopped for breath, Felicia noticed with satisfaction that Marilyn was speaking to Joyce in the same tone of voice that Joyce used with Felicia. Joyce was a year and a half younger than Marilyn.

"Prime Ribs *de Boeuf au Jus*," Felicia read the menu.

"Roast beef," said Marshall. "I know that."

"*Pommes de Terre Rôti*," Felicia shouted, since the band had started to play the "Anniversary Waltz" right over their heads.

"*Carottes Belges*," she went on.

"Carrots," snorted Marshall.

Josh and Barbara got up and danced to the Anniversary Waltz. Everybody clapped, and then some more people started dancing.

Marilyn looked toward the head table expectantly. The usher she had been talking to got up, and Marilyn looked like she was ready to leap out of her chair.

He turned to the bridesmaid next to him and led her out onto the dance floor. Marilyn slumped back in her seat.

Felicia wanted to hold her hands over her ears. She thought she was going to be deaf by the time the wedding was over. The music actually began to hurt, and she could feel the thumps of the bass fiddle right in her stomach.

"Hey, Marshall, let's dance," Felicia suggested as the band played a loud fast number.

"Nah," said Marshall, "I don't want to."

"Oh, come *on*," Felicia said impatiently, yanking his arm as she stood up. "We can get away from the band for a while."

Josh came over to their table and asked Marilyn to dance. Marilyn jumped up eagerly. Felicia noticed, as she dragged Marshall out onto the dance floor, that her sister was talking rapidly to Josh and glancing over toward the head table.

Felicia danced with Marshall, who really could

dance very well, bouncing in time to the rock number, which seemed to go on forever. By the time it finally ended, Felicia was panting and perspiring.

She staggered back to the table, just as Josh came up behind her.

"Hi, Felicia!" he said. "Having a good time?"

"Oh yes," she panted politely, "very nice."

"How about a dance?"

Felicia stared in awe at her tall, handsome cousin with the beautiful brown eyes. She really just wanted to sink down into her chair and rest, but this was the *groom* asking her to dance! It's an honor, she told herself proudly.

"I'd love to," Felicia said, hoping the band would play something slow.

But they didn't. They started another rock number, and Felicia groaned inwardly and tried to catch her breath before she and Josh got back to the center of the floor.

Josh was a good dancer too, and when they danced, everybody watched them, and applauded when the music stopped and Josh led Felicia back to her table.

"Look," said Marshall, pointing to her plate. "Baked Alaska."

Baked Alaska! Felicia loved baked Alaska, but of course, she hardly ever had it unless there were some big, special occasion, like a wedding where it was served. And now she was too tired and too full from all the other food to eat it. She took a spoonful, and that was all she could manage to taste.

She suddenly felt sleepy and irritable. She was positive she was going deaf. Her ears were ringing. The accordion player was now singing, "I Could Have Danced All Night," and he still had a terrible voice.

Too much noise, Felicia thought resentfully, and we have to sit right next to it because we're kids. And funny-tasting punch. Her criticisms were beginning to pile up as she got tireder. She noticed Marilyn walking back to the table with the usher she'd been talking to before.

She's in love, Felicia thought suddenly. Desiree is in love! And she can't even sit with him!

"Do you have a pencil?" she asked Marshall abruptly.

He rummaged around in his pockets and came up with a ball-point pen that had "Sullivan's Girdles and Foundation Garments" printed on it.

"What are you doing?" he shouted as Felicia began to scribble on the back of the little menu card.

"Writing down some constructive criticism," Felicia shouted back irritably.

A little later, Josh and Barbara and their parents came around to the children's table to have a picture taken.

"And how are you enjoying yourselves?" Felicia's Aunt Marjorie asked.

"Very nice, thank you," Felicia said, covering up the menu she was writing on with her hand.

"What's that?" asked Barbara, pointing at the menu. "Have we a budding poet here?"

"Oh, no," Felicia stammered. "It's nothing."

"Oh, come on, let's see what you're writing," Aunt Marjorie teased, and snatched the menu from under Felicia's fingers.

"Please let me have it back!" Felicia begged. But her aunt was already reading the list to herself. Her face darkened. The bride's mother looked over Aunt Marjorie's shoulder, and her eyes grew narrow.

Don't put children's table right under band, they were reading. *They will go deaf. Have Coke instead of funny-tasting punch in dolphin. Have microphones in chapel so you can hear the wedding. Have smallest people sit in front so they can see the wedding. No pea soup. Let the ushers sit with who they want. Have more time before the wedding so people can eat the canapes and things. Don't let accordion player sing. Smaller dinner so people have room for baked Alaska.*

Felicia slumped miserably in her seat. From beneath her lowered eyelids she saw her mother, who was dancing with her father, look over at the children's table as if wondering what was going on. Then a look of horror came over her mother's face, and she stopped dancing and seemed to be about to race over in their direction. Her father took her firmly in his arms and danced her away.

"It's constructive criticism," Marshall explained helpfully.

Marilyn gaped at Felicia.

"We can see that," said Barbara's mother coldly.

Josh tried to look very stern and disapproving, but the corners of his mouth kept twitching and his eyes crinkled when he looked at Felicia.

The photographer hustled them all into place for the picture.

"Everybody say 'Meatballs,'" said the photographer, trying to make them laugh. Felicia couldn't even smile.

The bridal group, led by Barbara's mother, stalked off to the next table, without another word.

"How could you, Felicia!" Marilyn fumed, reaching over Joyce to grasp Felicia's wrist.

"But I didn't!" Felicia protested. "They grabbed it. I wasn't going to show — "

"You shouldn't have been writing it at all!" Marilyn hissed. "Oh, I've *never* been so *embarrassed*. . . ."

In the car going home, Felicia tried several times to explain to her mother what had happened.

"Not another word!" her mother kept shrieking. "Not one more word out of you!"

All the way home she raged at her. Felicia, exhausted and perspiring in the back seat, stopped trying to explain. Her mother didn't want an explanation, Felicia thought resentfully, she just wanted to yell.

"If you ever — EVER — do anything like this again," her mother threatened.

"I didn't do anything," Felicia mumbled tiredly to herself.

"I'll never see him again," Marilyn moaned softly, from her corner in the back seat. "He lives in Brooklyn. . . ."

"The end of the world," her father agreed.

"Brooklyn," Marilyn repeated hollowly.

Felicia fell, uncomfortably, to sleep.

8

"Now, remember," said Cheryl as they rang Phyllis's doorbell, "what you promised."

"I'll remember," Felicia replied soberly.

She had thought to herself that it wouldn't be much fun being a part of a club where you weren't allowed to make any suggestions, but that was the condition under which Phyllis, Lorraine and Fern had agreed to take Felicia as a member. Oh, Cheryl hadn't exactly *said* that Felicia wasn't allowed to open her mouth if she wanted to stay in the club, but Felicia was sure that was what they'd meant.

"It's just," Cheryl had explained haltingly, "that they don't like it when you criticize all the time. They feel sort of, well —"

It was kind of humiliating, Felicia thought, to join a club that made a special rule just for you, and at first she was tempted to tell them, "Who needs your stupid club?"

But pondering on it for a while, she began to worry

that once Cheryl joined, her best friends would be Phyllis, Lorraine and Fern, and she'd have no time for Felicia any more. So Felicia had promised not to be critical, not to question anyone's ideas, and to be a loyal, enthusiastic club member. She was joining really, not because she wanted to be part of the club so much, but because she was afraid of being left out.

And besides, she'd told herself bitterly, her career as a constructive critic had come to an abrupt halt after the wedding. Her mother was so cool and distant to her that Felicia went around for two days feeling as if there were a cold, hard stone in the pit of her stomach. Desiree went back to being Marilyn, although she still called herself Desiree, and was nastier and more sarcastic than ever. Even her father had given her an occasional disapproving look, and shook his head in bewilderment.

Hearing what the other girls in the club thought about her constructive criticism was the final blow. Felicia's vow to keep quiet was very sincere. Look where constructive criticism had gotten her! Feeling friendless and familyless, Felicia had toyed with the idea of never saying another word as long as she lived. At least that would keep people from hating her.

But, she reminded herself, she might have to talk in school, if the teacher asked her a question, or at home, if she wanted second helpings of spaghetti. So she decided not to do anything quite so drastic as never talking again, but just speak when it was necessary, and forget about constructive criticism entirely.

"Oh, hi," Phyllis said, flinging open the door. "Everyone's here already; we were waiting for you."

She led Felicia and Cheryl upstairs to her room.

Felicia thought it was the most beautiful room she'd ever seen. The walls were painted bright pink. The curtains were white and looked sheer and airy. The bedspread was a mass of pink and red roses and there was a shaggy white rug on the floor. Phyllis's furniture was white, and she had white wicker chairs with pink and red cushions.

Felicia's own room was furnished with solid, sturdy maple furniture, and had a plain muted plaid bedspread. She felt a pang of envy as she looked around Phyllis's room.

"Well," said Phyllis briskly, "now that we're all here, we can start the meeting. I think the first thing we should do is elect officers."

What's the name of this club? Felicia asked herself.

"Don't you think we should pick the name first, Phyllis?" Fern asked doubtfully.

There, Felicia thought with satisfaction. I'm not the only one who makes suggestions.

"We'll pick the name after we choose the officers," Phyllis replied decisively. "We have to have a president to take charge of the meeting first."

"So she can pick the name herself," Fern grumbled.

"Nominations for president," Phyllis announced.

"I nominate Phyllis Brody," Lorraine said importantly.

"Now someone has to second me — I mean the nomination," Phyllis said.

"I second," Cheryl said in a low voice.

Felicia glanced over at her curiously, but Cheryl didn't even look up.

"Any other nominations?" Phyllis asked confidently.

No one said a word.

"Now we'll vote. All in favor — "

"Shouldn't we have a secret ballot?" Fern suggested.

"Why?" Phyllis asked blankly. "I'm the only candidate."

Felicia listened silently as the other officers were elected, only raising her hand to vote along with the others. President, Phyllis. Vice-President, Cheryl. Secretary, Fern. Treasurer, Lorraine.

"I think," Cheryl said suddenly, "that Felicia ought to be something too. It isn't fair for her to be the only person who isn't an officer."

"But there aren't any more offices," Lorraine pointed out.

"I don't think it's fair," Cheryl insisted stubbornly.

Felicia plucked uneasily at the shaggy rug.

"All right," Phyllis sighed. "She can be sergeant-at-arms."

"What's that?" asked Cheryl curiously.

"She helps to keep order at the meetings. She throws out the troublemakers."

Oh, great, Felicia thought unhappily. Since I'm the only troublemaker around, as far as they're concerned, I'll probably have to throw myself out some day. No I won't, she vowed. I'm not a troublemaker any more.

"Well — " said Cheryl.

But Phyllis had settled the question and was already beginning a discussion of the club's name.

"Now we have had a couple of suggestions," Phyllis said. "One was 'Daughters of Athena.' "

Yucchh, Felicia said, but only to herself.

"Yuck," said Lorraine, echoing her thoughts.

Felicia grinned, but seeing Phyllis's angry face, quickly resumed a serious, attentive expression.

"Some other suggestions have been 'Jabogs,' " Phyllis went on, saying "Jabogs" as if the name had a nasty smell, "and 'Plainvillettes.' "

Sounds like we're a bunch of baton twirlers, Felicia thought.

"There are five of us," Fern said thoughtfully.

"How about something like 'The Fabulous Five'?"

"Or the 'Friendly Five,'" Lorraine suggested.

If we were that friendly, Felicia thought, there'd be more than five of us.

"Hey!" Lorraine said excitedly, "you know what would be good? Five-F. You know, five of us, and we could be Friendly, Fabulous, Funny, Fearless and — and — " She groped for another word that began with F.

Feeble-minded, thought Felicia. She tried not to giggle.

"Doesn't that remind you of the 4-H clubs?" Phyllis asked dubiously.

"That's what makes it so good," Lorraine insisted.

Felicia couldn't understand that at all.

"Fine?" suggested Cheryl. "No, that's no good."

"Frank?" asked Fern. "You know, like honest."

"Good! Frank is good!" Lorraine said enthusiastically.

"All right," Phyllis shrugged. "We'll take a vote. All in favor of 'Daughters of Athena' say aye."

Phyllis's was the only "aye." She looked around, disturbed, waiting for the others to back her up, but this time, Felicia saw happily, they were standing up to her. Felicia was glad, because she'd hate to have to tell people the name of the club she belonged to was "Daughters of Athena." The other girls were probably thinking the same thing.

"One vote," Phyllis said curtly. "All in favor of JABOGS?"

Lorraine, whose idea it was, started to raise her hand tentatively, but changed her mind.

"No votes," said Phyllis smugly. "All in favor of the Five-F's?"

Everyone but Phyllis yelled, "Aye!"

"Okay," she shrugged. "Five-F's is the name of our club."

There was a knock on the door, and Phyllis's mother came in carrying a tray of little sandwiches and potato chips, cookies and Cokes. The girls descended on the food as if they hadn't eaten all week.

"Now," said Phyllis a little while later, "we have to decide on dues. How much do you think they should be?"

What do we need dues for? Felicia wondered.

"Do we have to have dues?" Lorraine asked.

"Of course," Phyllis replied. "What if we need to buy something, or want money for a trip or something like that?"

"Then we could all bring our own money, or chip in a certain amount when we need something," Cheryl said.

"All clubs have dues," Phyllis declared firmly. "Now, how much do you think they should be?"

"A quarter a week?" Fern suggested meekly.

"A quarter a week!" Phyllis snorted. "That won't even buy us Cokes for our meetings!"

"Fifty cents?" Lorraine said reluctantly.

"I was thinking of one dollar a meeting," Phyllis said.

"One dollar a week!" Lorraine squealed. "My allowance is only two-fifty!"

"Oh, well, mine is five," Phyllis said casually.

They finally compromised on seventy-five cents a meeting. Felicia quickly figured in her head that that was three dollars a month, or four-fifty if the month had five weeks. That would be more than a whole week's allowance to pay, just to belong to a club where she wasn't allowed to say anything. If it weren't for Cheryl . . . Felicia sighed.

"You know," Phyllis began thoughtfully, "we could do something to raise money so we'll have funds in our treasury right away. It'll take us a long time to save up anything if we only collect three seventy-five a week and use part of that for refreshments."

"How could we raise money?" Fern asked.

"We could raffle off something," Phyllis mused.

"What?" Lorraine asked scornfully. "We haven't got anything to raffle off."

"Maybe we could get some local store to donate something," Cheryl suggested.

"Oh, no," Lorraine scoffed. "They only do that for good causes. We're not a good cause. Why should they give us anything for free?"

"That's true," Phyllis agreed, wrinkling up her forehead.

"We could have a carnival," Fern said, "and make games and give prizes and charge admission and everything."

Who's going to pay for the prizes? Felicia wondered.

"That sounds good," Phyllis nodded.

"Where would you have it?" asked Lorraine.

"We could use my backyard," offered Phyllis. "My mother wouldn't mind."

In the *winter?* Felicia thought incredulously.

"You know," Cheryl began, "there are only five of us. If one of us takes the admission tickets, that leaves only four to run the games. Four games isn't very much."

What if it snows? Felicia's inner voice persisted.

"Oh, we could have more than four," Phyllis said reassuringly. "We could go from booth to booth — we could each handle two booths if they were close together."

Or sleets, Felicia went on, to herself.

But incredibly, no one mentioned the weather. Phyllis and Fern were so excited about the idea of a carnival that their enthusiasm infected even the doubtful Cheryl and Lorraine. Felicia writhed on the wicker chair in agonized silence. She was sure this was a bad idea; she knew it in her bones, and she could see a hundred things that could go wrong. It could rain. It could snow. Where would they get enough prizes? Who was going to make the booths, and with what? How were they going to keep the kids out of Phyllis's yard until they paid admission? The yard had no fence on the sides, only along the back. If it was cold and snowy or raining, who was going to let their little kids outside to come to the carnival in the first place?

No, Felicia wanted to yell, don't do it! You'll be sorry! It's going to be terrible!

She gnawed on her lips to keep from opening her mouth. She dug her fingernails into her palms to remind herself of her promise. If they want to have a disaster, Felicia told herself firmly, that's their business. They said they didn't want any suggestions. They said they didn't like me to criticize their ideas all the time. I *promised*. What do *I* care what happens to this dumb club, anyway?

But it was torture for Felicia to keep quiet when she

knew that a little constructive criticism could avert disaster. Even though she didn't care what happened to the club, she kept thinking to herself, someone should *say* something. *Someone* should warn them. Was it fair to let them go on and on, do all that work, and count on a big, successful carnival when she *knew* it was bound to be a failure? Didn't she have a *duty* to point out what was wrong with their plan? How could she sit here and let them plunge into this, without saying a word? She was torn between keeping her promise, or saving them all from disappointment. What should she do? she wondered frantically.

"Okay," said Phyllis, "that's settled. It'll be a carnival. Now, we'll each be in charge of thinking up two games, and getting the equipment for them. Let's make a list of what we'll have."

A promise is a promise, Felicia told herself.

"We can have penny pitching," Lorraine said.

"And squirting out a candle with a water gun," Fern added.

It's their own fault, Felicia continued to herself. They were the ones who said I had to keep my mouth shut.

"And throwing beanbags through a clown face," Cheryl said.

"And tossing rings around Coke bottles," Phyllis

said, scribbling furiously to keep up with the suggestions.

"We should have a fortune-teller," Fern said suddenly. "Dressed up like a gypsy."

"Oh, I want to do that!" Lorraine exclaimed.

"No, it was my idea," Fern protested. "I should be the fortune-teller."

Felicia sipped fitfully at her Coke. She wouldn't say anything, she decided. She'd made a promise in order to be in this club, and if she expected to *stay* in, she'd better keep her promise.

But, she wondered, why do I *want* to stay in it? She had joined a club in which no one paid the slightest attention to her, where she sat, mute and unparticipating for almost an hour and a half. She had joined the club so she wouldn't feel left out of Cheryl's activities, but she wondered how she could possibly have felt more left out if she'd never joined the club at all.

9

". . . and the winds are from the northwest at fifteen to twenty miles an hour. The temperature is nineteen W G V M degrees."

Felicia glanced automatically at the window thermometer. She started to say, "Twenty-one," but glancing at her sister she changed it to "Brr!"

Marilyn smiled contentedly.

"It's going to be an awfully cold day for a carnival," Felicia's mother said, shaking her head.

"I know," Felicia agreed ruefully. "That's what I thought in the first place."

She poked her scrambled eggs around the plate. The Five-F's had been working for weeks to get ready for the carnival. Felicia was in charge of preparing the penny-pitch and the bottle ring-toss. She'd collected Coke bottles from everybody until she had enough to fill a wooden crate. Then she'd cut out rings from plastic can lids, making sure that they'd fit over the tops of the bottles.

For the penny-pitch, she'd found an old, galvanized iron washtub in the basement, that had once belonged to her grandmother. She was going to fill it with water, and put three saucers on the bottom. If a penny landed in any one of the saucers, the person won a prize. Felicia practiced pitching pennies into it that way, and it was difficult enough so that people wouldn't win very often, but so it was still possible to do it.

She'd made two signs, on big pieces of posterboard, for the games, and had gotten a folding card table from her mother to use for the bottle-toss. The penny-pitch basin could be right on the ground, although she didn't know where she was going to put the sign for it. Maybe she could take one of the folding chairs that went with the card table, and tape the sign to the back of it, and put that right behind the basin. *If* her father could get all that into the car.

"It's ridiculous to have a carnival in the middle of winter, you know," Marilyn said indifferently.

"I know," replied Felicia.

"You're going to freeze out there," Marilyn warned.

"Probably," Felicia agreed glumly.

It was amazing, she thought, that in all those weeks they were preparing for the carnival, no one noticed that it was definitely winter. Of course, it hadn't snowed yet, so maybe that was why it had never occurred to any of the other Five-F's that it *might* snow on the day of their carnival. But the days had been getting colder and colder. Even Felicia finally had to admit that it had become too cold to wear her reindeer sweater without a coat over it.

Well, she thought, at least it's sunny out, so they won't have to worry about sleet or snow.

Cheryl called a little later to tell Felicia she'd be late getting to the carnival. After her French class at the Cultural Arts Community Workshop, her mother was taking her to audition for a new music teacher, who only took the most promising students. But she was sure she could be at Phyllis's by one-thirty at the latest.

After Cheryl called, Felicia actually began to look forward to the carnival. In the warmth of her own house, it was hard to keep on worrying about how cold it was outside. The weeks of work and preparation, making posters to put up around the neighborhood, and the enthusiasm of the rest of the Five-F's had infected her. Felicia felt a mounting excitement as the morning dragged slowly on. After all, it would be fun running a carnival! She liked little kids, and she liked the idea of being in charge of her games.

At lunch time, Felicia gobbled down her sandwich and soup and ran off to collect her equipment.

"Two sweaters, Felicia!" her mother yelled after her. "And button them!"

"Okay!" she called back, dragging the tub and the saucers up from the basement. The case of empty bottles was in the garage, where her father would put it in the trunk of the car. The rings were around the necks of the Coke bottles, so she wouldn't forget them.

Felicia put on two sweaters, her parka with a hood, and wool mittens. She wrapped her long blue and yellow wool scarf around her neck.

"I'm ready," she said, coming into the kitchen where her father was still sitting with his lunch. She stood next to him, silently, bundled up so she could hardly move, and watched him eat. Her eyes reproached him for dawdling over his food when she was so unbearably eager to get going.

"All right, all right!" he cried finally, and pushed his plate away. "I give up!"

"I didn't say anything," Felicia remarked innocently, but she beamed as he went to the front closet to get his coat.

It took a little while to pile everything into the car, but finally they got it all organized and drove off. Felicia actually felt a little warm in the car, although when she'd first stepped out of her house the shock of the whipping wind had taken her breath away.

"It's not so cold," she commented brightly as they drove up to Phyllis's house.

Her father switched off the car heater and stopped in the driveway.

There was a beautifully colored poster taped to Phyllis's front door.

CARNIVAL TODAY! 2 PM
GAMES, PRIZES!!
FORTUNE TELLER!!
(AROUND BACK)
ADMISSION: 25¢

They took the things into the backyard, where Phyllis and Fern were already busy working. They were bundled up too, and their breath came out like streamers of smoke in front of their faces.

"I wish Cheryl and Lorraine would get here," Phyllis fumed. "We really haven't got much time."

"Oh," Felicia remembered, "Cheryl said to tell you she'll be a little late. She has to audition for a bass teacher."

"Of all days!" Phyllis groaned, clapping her gloved hands together to try and keep warm.

"Do you think," Fern gasped, hugging herself as she moved from one foot to the other, "that your mother would let us have the carnival in the basement?"

"No," Phyllis objected, "that's no good. We haven't got nearly enough room down there."

"But nobody will see my gypsy costume," Fern wailed. "How can I be a gypsy fortune-teller if no one can see my gypsy costume under my coat?"

"Well," Phyllis said, eyeing her, "you've got your scarf and earrings, that'll just have to do. And we can see your long dress," she added soothingly, "even under the coat."

"And you could put your shawl on over your coat," Felicia added.

Fern was still not convinced, and grumbled as she set up her tent, made out of a big sheet and two badminton net poles.

"This keeps blowing off!" she wailed as she tried to get the sheet to stay up.

"Go inside and ask my father for some tacks," Phyllis said, as she and Felicia set up her folding table.

Mr. Brody came out to help them, and tacked the ends of the sheets to the tops of the poles.

"I hope these stay up," he said doubtfully, patting one of the poles gently. "The ground was so hard, I couldn't pound them in very far."

"Oh, they'll be okay," Phyllis said confidently.

Fern had a little table between the two poles, and she had taped a sign to it which read,

MADAME ZALONGA:
FORTUNES TOLD, 50¢

The sign flapped a lot in the wind, and the whole thing didn't look very much like a tent at all, Felicia thought, but Phyllis reassured Fern, "It's just the idea of a tent, that's all you need."

Mr. Brody and Felicia went back and forth several times to the house, hauling pails of water to pour into Felicia's penny-pitch tub. Felicia wanted to use the garden hose, but Mr. Brody said the outside water was turned off for the winter so the pipes wouldn't freeze.

Lorraine arrived and they helped her set up the beanbag toss and the magnetic dart board. They nailed the dart board to a tree, and leaned the clown face with the holes for beanbags to go through against the back wall of Phyllis's house. They fumbled through gloved fingers with the Scotch tape to put up the sign on the house above the painted plywood clown.

Cheryl rushed in at last, breathless and red-cheeked, with her water pistol, candle, and a pack of matches.

She only had to run one game, because she was going to be taking the admission money.

It was nearly two o'clock. Everything was ready. Phyllis had set up a shooting gallery on the redwood barbecue table by taping a row of cardboard ducks to it so they stuck upright; she had borrowed her little brother's popgun, which shot corks, to use to shoot the ducks.

They each took a small supply of prizes, which were party favors they had bought at the supermarket to give out to the winners. They had used almost all the money in the club treasury to buy the prizes.

A little boy wandered into the yard.

"Hey, you better go stand on the side," Phyllis told Cheryl, "and take their money. We don't want them coming in without paying."

Cheryl went off to stand where they figured the admission gate ought to be.

"It costs a quarter to come in, little boy," Phyllis said, "and a quarter for each game."

The boy dug into his snowsuit pocket and pulled out a dollar, which he handed to Phyllis.

"Go give it to that girl over there," she pointed. "She's in charge of taking the money."

Obediently, the boy trotted over to Cheryl and handed her the dollar.

"Hey!" Cheryl called. "I haven't any change!"

"Oh, no," groaned Phyllis, "I never thought of that!"

"Why don't you play some games," Felicia suggested, "and if you play three games, that'll be a dollar."

"Okay," the boy said agreeably. He went over to the dart board first, but none of the darts even landed on the target, they just fell down under the tree.

He got three tries at the beanbag toss, but none of his beanbags went through any of the holes in the clown's face.

Finally he went over to Cheryl's candle and said, "I want to do this. What do you have to do?"

"You have to shoot the water pistol at the candle and squirt the flame out," Phyllis explained.

"But it's not lit," he pointed out.

Cheryl came racing over to her booth.

"You'd better light the candle," Phyllis said. "He wants to try."

Cheryl fumbled through her mittens with the matches, and finally got one lit, but the wind immediately blew it out. She tried again, then took off her mittens so it would be easier. Finally, she got the candle lit.

The little boy grabbed the water gun and squirted

at the candle. Just as he did, the wind blew the flame out.

"I win, I win!" he yelled. "Where's my prize?"

"You didn't shoot that anywhere near the candle!" Cheryl protested. "The wind blew it out. Look, here's where you hit." She pointed to a wet streak on the table.

"I did so win!" he howled. "I put the light out! I want my prize!"

Three more children came into the yard.

"All right, all right," Phyllis grumbled. "Here, here's a prize." She handed him a little plastic monkey.

Cheryl ran over to the three children to get their admission money.

"I want to play that," the little boy said, pointing to Felicia's penny-pitch.

"Do you have any pennies?" Felicia asked him. "You need a penny to throw into one of those plates."

"Just my dollar," he said, searching through his pockets. "They took my dollar."

He ran up to Cheryl. "I want my change now!" he yelled. "I gave you a dollar."

"But you used up your dollar," Cheryl said, "playing the games."

"I want my change! You told me it was only a quarter!"

Cheryl looked helplessly over at Phyllis. The three children who had come in were at three different booths, and one was beginning to complain that the wind made her dart miss the target.

Phyllis rushed over to Cheryl and the boy.

"Now look, little boy," she said sternly, squatting down to look him in the eye, "you used up all your money. You don't get any change. Now stop yelling."

But he didn't. Finally he began to cry. Howling, "I'm going to tell my mother!" he ran out of the yard.

More children had found their way to the carnival in the meanwhile, and Felicia was very busy running between her two games. Everybody seemed to be winning the ring-the-bottle, and she looked down at her small pile of prizes, growing dangerously smaller. She wondered if she had made the rings too big.

Their signs began to flap in the wind, and one of Felicia's ripped off and flew across the yard. The wind was biting, and Felicia stamped her feet and clapped her hands together to try to keep warm. The ends of her scarf kept flying across her face.

"I can't keep this lit!" Cheryl wailed. "I used up a whole pack of matches already!" There was a line of kids waiting to play the candle-squirt game, and Cheryl looked frantic.

The water in Felicia's penny-pitch basin was beginning to turn icy around the rim of the tub. Just looking at it made Felicia colder. What if it froze, with all the pennies at the bottom? Would she have to chop away the ice to dig out the money?

Suddenly she noticed three bigger boys climbing over the back of the fence.

"Hey!" she yelled. "You can't come in that way! It costs a quarter to get in!"

But they ignored her, and everybody else was so busy trying to run two booths at once, that they paid no attention to the gate-crashers.

"The wind blew that away!" one boy was saying to Felicia after he finished his three ring-tosses. "That's not fair; I want to do that one over again."

"Three chances for a quarter," Felicia said firmly. "No do-overs."

"It's not fair!" he repeated angrily.

"Fake!" Felicia heard someone yell. She looked around, and saw a little girl standing next to Fern's fortune-telling tent, or at least, what was left of it. One of the poles was practically blown down, and Fern's sheet was whipping around her. The little girl was pointing an accusing finger at her as she cried, "You're not Madame Zalonga; you're *Fern!*"

The wind ripped off three more signs and flung them out of the yard. The dart board clattered around so against the tree that the kids who weren't complaining about the wind blowing their darts off course were yelling that someone should hold the dart board still, or else it wasn't fair.

Over at the shooting gallery Phyllis had to give almost everyone a prize, because the ducks bobbed and bounced every time the wind blew, and all the kids insisted that they had hit them with the cork gun, because they moved, didn't they?

Just as Felicia ran out of prizes completely, the little boy who had been their first customer came back, dragging his mother by the arm. She was wearing a wool scarf over pink rollers, and looked very angry.

"How could you take money from a child?" the woman demanded of a puzzled Cheryl.

"We didn't take money from him!" Cheryl replied. "He spent it."

"He says he gave you a dollar and you didn't give him any change."

"He spent his change," Cheryl tried to explain. "On the games."

"He says you owe him change," the woman insisted angrily, "and my child does not lie!"

"Well, maybe he just doesn't know much about money," Cheryl retorted.

"He knows enough to know when he's been cheated!" the boy's mother shouted. "And he says you cheated him."

A frenzied Phyllis came rushing over. "Don't argue with her," she told Cheryl. "We haven't got the time. Give the kid three quarters."

"But," Cheryl objected indignantly, "that's not right!"

Phyllis dug three quarters out of her pocket and nearly threw them at the woman.

"We're out of prizes," Phyllis said frantically as Cheryl, Fern and Felicia huddled around her. "We're going to have to make these kids wait until my father gets back from the store with more."

They looked around. There were kids all over, screaming for their turns at the games.

"And the cork from the popgun blew away," Phyllis went on despairingly, "and they have nothing to shoot with."

"I owe two kids prizes," Felicia said. She hopped up and down, desperately trying to keep warm. She could hardly feel her toes any more.

"I think I'm getting frostbite," Fern whimpered. "How can mothers let their kids out in this kind of weather, anyway?"

They looked bleakly around the yard. One boy had just pushed a little girl into the icy water of the penny-pitch, and she was screaming as she ran off to tell her mother. A fistfight had broken out in front of the dart game, over whose turn it was to go, and Lorraine was gingerly trying to separate the two boys without getting clobbered.

"You know something?" Fern said suddenly, her voice hoarse and wretched. "I'm freezing. And I don't think this carnival is such a good idea anymore."

Felicia thought Fern looked as if she were about to cry.

Phyllis bit her lip. The whole thing did seem to be getting out of hand. Somehow, with the wind blowing everything over, and not enough of them to watch all the children at once, and two of the games gone because of the weather . . .

"Hey!" Felicia yelled. "It's snowing!"

They looked up. Big, fluffy flakes were beginning to drift down, but blown by the wind into their red faces, the snow felt like a blizzard.

Felicia felt a rush of excitement as she always did when it snowed for the first time in the winter. She would have forgotten all about how cold she was and what a disaster the carnival was, if the kids hadn't started shouting, "It's snowing! It's snowing!" and running wildly around the yard.

"That does it," Phyllis said grimly. "We might as well send them home."

Half of the kids were so excited by the snow, they were already running out of the yard to go home, but when Phyllis announced that the carnival was closed, there were howls of protest.

"I didn't get my prize! You promised me a prize!"

"It was my turn! I want my turn!"

"I just *got* here! I didn't get to play anything! I paid a *quarter!*"

"All right, all right!" Phyllis shouted. "You'll get your prizes as soon as they get here. But the carnival is closed. No more games."

"But I paid a quarter! And I didn't play *anything!*"

"So did I!" three others chorused.

"You'll get your quarters back," Phyllis said.

Just then her father came hurrying into the yard with a bag.

"I got as many as I could," he said, handing the bag to Phyllis, "with the money you gave me."

"Oh, great," Phyllis sighed, "and we're closing up now."

"Too bad," he said sympathetically. He looked around the ravaged yard. "This is going to be some mess to clean up."

"I know, I know," Phyllis grumbled. She handed out prizes to the kids who said they had won them. They all finally went home, and Phyllis was left with three quarters of the bag still full.

"You must be frozen," Mr. Brody said. "Look, go on inside and warm up a little. I'll help you with this later."

"I have to get my mother's bridge table and chair," Felicia shivered. "She wouldn't like them to get snowed on."

"All right, I'll bring in the good tables," he said. "Now go on, you just go inside."

They rushed indoors gratefully and clustered in the kitchen, coats and gloves still on, trying to get warm. Mrs. Brody took one look at them, and put up a big pot of milk to heat for cocoa. They all tried to hold their hands over the stove at once.

"Take your coats off," she advised. "You can't get warm with your coats on."

No one listened to her. It just didn't seem logical, Felicia thought, to take your coat *off* to get warm.

Finally they trooped up to Phyllis's room. Mrs. Brody followed behind them with cookies and the tray of cocoa cups.

Dejected, Phyllis flopped on the bed and emptied out her pockets. "We might as well count the money," she said.

They put all the money they had collected on the bed.

"I had to give my father five dollars for more prizes," Phyllis said. "I took it out of Cheryl's admission money and Lorraine's and my games." She counted up what they had spilled onto the bed.

"Five dollars and fifteen cents," she announced

wearily. "Plus the money in the penny-pitch. How much is in there?"

"Not much," Felicia replied. "Maybe ten cents." And we might, Felicia thought ruefully, have to wait for the spring thaw to get *that* out.

"Five dollars and twenty-five cents for all that work!" Lorraine groaned. "We must have spent more than that just on posters and paint."

"And making the games," Fern added bitterly.

"And the prizes!" Lorraine remembered. "They ate up our treasury, and half our profit!"

"Why didn't we think of the weather?" Phyllis moaned. "And why didn't we get more people to help us?"

Felicia sipped her cocoa and nibbled on a cookie. She wasn't glad that she had been right; as a matter of fact, she was beginning to think the carnival had been a good idea, but it just needed to be run a little more *efficiently*. And in better weather.

"Why didn't someone *think?*" Phyllis cried dramatically, clapping her hand to her forehead.

Suddenly their heads turned toward Felicia. She was startled as she saw the accusing looks on their faces. She cast her eyes downward into her cocoa cup.

"Felicia," Phyllis began slowly, "you're always criticizing everything. Why didn't you think up all the things that could go wrong *this* time?"

"Yes, Felicia," Lorraine continued angrily, "how come *this* time you were so quiet all of a sudden?"

"That's not fair," Cheryl objected. "Maybe she didn't think of the things that could go wrong. W*e* didn't."

"Yes, but *she* always does," Fern said. "I'll bet she saw what was wrong with the carnival, and just didn't tell us."

Felicia could feel the angry stares, even though she was still looking down into her cocoa.

"I was going to tell you," she began slowly, "but I promised not to say anything. Cheryl told me I had to not criticize anything if I wanted to be in the club."

"See," Lorraine said triumphantly. "She *did* know all along!"

"I wanted to tell you," Felicia said soberly, "but I promised."

"Oh, for heaven's sake, Felicia," Phyllis said, exasperated. "The *one time* we needed some — "

"It's your own fault," Cheryl said suddenly. "You were the ones who didn't want any criticism."

Felicia looked at her friend. She could still depend on Cheryl, she thought fondly.

"You know," Cheryl said, "it's not everybody who can see when things are going to go wrong. W*e* didn't. It must be a talent, to be able to know when an idea is not going to work or to see the mistakes in things."

Felicia glowed with pleasure.

"I think you should listen to someone like that," Cheryl went on, "instead of trying to keep her quiet." She glanced around at the others. "That's all," she said abruptly, looking a little sheepish.

"I think it's a good idea," Felicia said suddenly. "The carnival, I mean. Only, maybe in the summer."

"Sure," Phyllis said pensively. "We can keep all the stuff we made, even the posters that didn't blow away."

"And we have all those prizes left over," Felicia pointed out. "And if we made even two dollars profit, in less than an hour, think of what we could make if we ran it all day."

"And maybe there'll be more people in the club then," Cheryl added, "so we'll have more help in running things."

Felicia finished off her cocoa with a contented sigh. She wasn't going to be a silent club member after all, she told herself with satisfaction. They had practically admitted they needed her constructive criticism, and even though they hadn't actually said so, Felicia was sure she was going to be allowed to speak from now on.

Perhaps, she thought, she had given up her career as a constructive critic too hastily.

10

Felicia took out her Criticism Notebook. It had been a while since she'd written in it, but after reading an editorial in the newspaper this evening, she'd been inspired to make a few notes.

"Desiree," she called, knocking at her sister's door, later, "could I have a piece of your stationery?"

"Okay," her sister said, opening the door. "But just one piece." She handed her a piece of letter paper with orange and yellow butterflies embossed in the corner.

"Could I have an envelope too, please?" Felicia asked.

Marilyn gave her an orange envelope, with butterflies on the flap.

"Thank you."

"You're welcome," her sister said, almost pleasantly.

But Felicia was too lost in thought to wonder about Marilyn's mood.

She hurried to her room and sat down at her desk.

Consulting her notes, she began to write as neatly as she could:

The President
The White House
Washington, D. C.

Dear Mr. President:
Even though I did not vote for you, I have a couple of suggestions I'd like to make to help you run the country a little better. . . .